FOR PRA

CW00371355

After the immediate shock of the deaths
of her beloved mother and stepfather,
Carol realised that her responsibility
now was to their little son Paul, and she
prepared to take him back to live with
her in England. But her stepfather's
nephew, Arturo Kane, had decided the
child should stay in California—with
him. Was Carol in a position to argue?

Books you will enjoy
by CLAUDIA JAMESON

YOURS . . . FAITHFULLY

Although she was rich, Cindy was anything but a playgirl; she was a very efficient and dedicated secretary. But when the dynamic Zac Stone took over the advertising agency where she worked, he seemed determined to think the worst of her. She would show him!

NEVER SAY NEVER

'You're not my type,' the dynamic Adam Francis had assured Jane Winters at their very first meeting—but that statement wasn't exactly borne out by his subsequent relentless pursuit of her! But for personal reasons, Jane just didn't want to get involved. Would she have the strength of mind to resist this man, who always got what he wanted?

THE MELTING HEART

Working as secretary to the formidable Comte Emile Jacquot de Nîmes was going to be particularly challenging for April Baxter because of the special circumstances involved. And then she had to complicate matters by falling in love with this man who would always be unattainable—because of Françoise . . .

LESSON IN LOVE

Once again Gina's father had let her down; he had always put his business life before her—and now, when she had come all the way to Africa to visit him, he had taken off again, leaving her stranded. So how *dared* that infuriating Alex Craig suggest that she was being wrong and childish to resent the situation? He could just mind his own business!

FOR PRACTICAL REASONS

BY
CLAUDIA JAMESON

MILLS & BOON LIMITED
15–16 BROOK'S MEWS
LONDON W1A 1DR

First published 1983
Australian copyright 1983
Philippine copyright 1983
This edition 1983

© Claudia Jameson 1983

ISBN 0 263 74354 3

Set in Monophoto Times 10 on 10½ pt.
01–1083 – 60847

Made and printed in Great Britain by
Richard Clay (The Chaucer Press) Ltd,
Bungay, Suffolk

For
my mother,
with much love

CHAPTER ONE

CAROL PALMER lowered her head, her eyes closing involuntarily against the scene which was taking place. Her heart was thumping violently, abnormally. The sound of it, the blood rushing against her eardrums, almost deafened her to the priest's words, words she was trying so hard to listen to, to take comfort from. Beyond the solitary voice there was silence, stillness, except for the murmur of the warm wind in the leaves of the nearby trees.

She opened her eyes, frowning against the glare of the afternoon sun as she glanced at the faces of the people surrounding the graveside. Most of them were total strangers to her, but they were people who had known and loved her mother and her stepfather, Ellen and Samuel Kane. Ellen and Sam were being buried, now, together.

Sam's nephew, someone else Carol hardly knew, stood motionless at her side. She didn't look at him, nor did she realise that the service was over, that the calm and steady voice had stopped speaking. There was a moment when the whole world seemed to shift sideways; cold perspiration trickled down her forehead, her ears were ringing and in her head there was a voice protesting over and over, 'No. No! *No!*'

A firm hand took a grip on her arm as she swayed on her feet. 'Carol? Come on, it's all over. It's time to go.'

She looked up at the man by her side, unable to make out what he had said. He towered over her by several inches, half shading her from the sun as he turned her away from the grave. His dark features blurred before her eyes and only then did she realise how close she was to fainting. But she wouldn't faint; she wasn't the fainting type. If she could just stand still a moment longer, she'd be all right. She wanted to tell the man this, but her voice came out in a harsh whisper and she heard herself saying something quite different. 'It seems so wrong ... It seems wrong that the sun can shine, that the sky can be so perfectly blue when ... when ... It makes me angry!'

Arturo Kane said nothing. His face swam before her eyes and she shook her head, realising how irrational she must have sounded. For seconds, just split seconds, Carol knew nothing but darkness. Still on her feet, she felt Arturo's arm around her waist. It was firm and strong, making her aware of her thinness as the hardness of it pressed against her lower ribs.

'I'm all right.' Even as she spoke she found herself leaning heavily against him. Her stepfather's nephew was a big man, far taller than she, and she was certainly tall enough. At five feet ten Carol did not meet many men who could dwarf her the way Arturo did.

'Take it easy,' he ordered, his arm tightening around her. 'Breathe deeply and rest against me. The sooner I get you into the car, the better.'

'Really, I'm all right.' Carol straightened at once. Neither literally nor figuratively was she in the habit of leaning on people. People usually leaned on her, depended on her strength.

Somehow she managed to thank everyone for attending, to accept the words of condolence and sympathy from those who would not be going back to her mother's house. Arturo did likewise; his voice, his stance, as steady as a rock as he kept one arm firmly around Carol's waist.

They turned, leading the entourage of mourners from the graveside to the waiting cars, the priest walking slowly by their side. She glanced at Sam's nephew, her voice coming out more curtly than she intended. 'I said I'm okay now, Arturo. Let me go, please.' Carol Palmer did not want to be seen to be weak. Weakness was something she sympathised with in other people but would not tolerate in herself. She made no allowances for the terrible emotions churning inside her, for the fact that she had not finished convalescing after her illness and had had to fly thousands of miles to attend her mother and stepfather's funeral. A little defiantly she raised her eyes to meet those of Arturo Kane.

He looked at her steadily, his eyes, as black as jet, narrowed slightly as he examined her face. And his arm stayed right where it was. 'I'll be the judge of that.'

The priest took his leave of them as they reached the cemetery gates. 'Miss Palmer—Dr Kane.' He shook hands with them and they thanked him warmly for all he had done.

Carol paused before walking to the car, her eyes sweeping over the magnificent view which could be seen to its best advantage from the high hillside on which they were standing. The city of San Francisco stretched out before her. San Francisco with its famous harbour, the Golden Gate Bridge, its endless hills. San Francisco—where her mother had been so very, very happy.

Carol lifted her hands to brush away the loosened strands of her dark brown hair. For years she had worn it the same way, parted down the centre and held in place at the nape. It was straight and plain, just as she was. But the wind was getting stronger now, making her efforts at control pointless. It was a warm wind, but in spite of that and the late April sunshine, she felt incredibly cold, chilled to the bone.

San Francisco ... America ... it was not Carol's own country, nor had it been her mother's. But Ellen had made it her own, Ellen had loved it, Ellen had ...

Nothing had changed.

Carol forced herself to acknowledge that fact and not to dwell upon thoughts of the accident which had snuffed out the lives of her mother and Sam, which had left their five-year-old son an orphan. That child, the product of her mother's second marriage, was lying in a coma. Somehow, miraculously, Paul had survived. The hospital in which he was being looked after was probably in Carol's view now, but she didn't know the city well enough to know in which direction it lay.

Thoughts of Paul made her hands curl tightly into fists. She must be strong. Now, more than ever, she must be strong. Life *does* go on. Before her, the city was throbbing with activity, vitality. There had been no silence, no stillness.

'Carol?' The arm around her waist tightened. 'If you're holding those tears in check for my benefit, don't. Let them go.'

She didn't answer him. She resented his intrusion. In the distance a ship's siren sounded, a deep bellow that carried on the wind. A plane cut its path in the clear blue sky overhead. For the rest of the world, nothing had changed. Only for Paul and for her would life be different from now on. And she would cope. Soon, she would take her little half-brother back to England and, somehow, she would cope. She had lived alone, fended for herself since she was eighteen. Now she was almost twenty-five and well equipped to bring up a child. Her new life would just need a little rearranging, that was all. Unconsciously, she squared her shoulders. Never yet had life presented her with a problem she couldn't deal with . . . But then never before had she been without her mother. No matter how far away, Ellen had always been there . . .

Carol's legs gave way beneath her and in the instant before darkness claimed her, she heard Arturo Kane curse softly beneath his breath.

She came to in stages. She could smell the faint tang of something fresh and masculine. She was lying down, cushioned by something leather. She was covered by something light and beneath her head there was something solid and warm. And she was in a car, a car in motion. Through its windows the sun was streaming, warming the lower half of her body.

'I'm so sorry.' Carol apologised automatically as she realised that her pillow was Arturo Kane's thigh and her blanket was the lightweight jacket he had been wearing.

He said nothing. He helped her into a sitting position as the driver drew the hired limousine to a halt outside the house. Barbie Howard, the neighbour who had kindly prepared food and drinks for everyone, was waiting by the garden gate. She took one look at Carol's face and flung the car door open before the driver had a chance to do it. 'Carol, honey, you look— come on, let me help you inside.'

'Is there any word from the hospital?' Carol got out very shakily, making no protest when Arturo helped her. Several other cars were lining the road as friends of Ellen and Sam arrived in convoy.

'No word.' Barbie stepped out of the way as Arturo steered Carol firmly towards the front door of the house. 'Was it . . . Art, did it . . .?'

'It was beautiful.' Arturo's voice was unusually soft. 'Thank you for staying here, Barbara. For all you've done.' As he stepped into the hall he advised Carol to go to her room and try to rest.

'Impossible.' She smiled weakly. 'First I must ring the hospital. Then—well, these people are my parents' friends . . .' What she was trying to say was that she felt it her duty to stay with them for a while.

'Skip this scene,' he said dismissively, watching her closely. 'You don't need it. You're not well, Carol. You've had pneumonia and you haven't fully recovered—contrary to what you told me. Now, will you take a doctor's advice and get some rest? If you caught another chill out there today, you're in trouble. I'll call the hospital. If there's anything to report, I'll come up and tell you.' He turned away from her, as if it were sufficient that he had told her what to do.

The fact that his advice was good didn't stop her resenting his attitude a little, but that was probably because he was a doctor, a psychiatrist, in fact. He was no doubt used to giving orders and having them acted upon without question. But Carol was far from foolhardy. She didn't believe in inviting trouble; she wouldn't neglect her health. She couldn't face food, but she was gasping for a hot drink and, more importantly, she really felt she ought to remain downstairs for a while. 'In an hour or so,' she said, her voice polite but firm. 'I'll rest when everyone's gone, Arturo.'

He glanced back at her as he headed for the kitchen, a somewhat speculative glint in his dark eyes. But he said nothing. After making the call to the hospital he came over to where Carol was sitting and told her there was nothing to report, that Paul's condition was unchanged, stable.

Immediately everyone left, she went to her room and Arturo went to his. Her body could be rested even if her mind couldn't. She hadn't slept for the past two nights, not since she had received Arturo's transatlantic phone call telling her of the tragedy. And she wouldn't sleep now, either. Unhappiness, worry and fear were churning around inside her, her mind was like a merry-go-round out of control as thoughts of the past, present and future whirled through it.

At least Ellen had had six good years, that was something to be thankful for, six gloriously happy years during which she had been married to Sam. Her first husband, Carol's father, had died when Carol was six months old. He had died young, suddenly, leaving Ellen with a hefty mortgage to pay and a child to bring up.

They had been so close, Carol and her mother. There had never been another man in Ellen's life. Perhaps it was because of that, the fact that it had always been just the two of them, that they had been more like sisters, friends, than mother and daughter. And Ellen had given birth to Carol at nineteen, so the age difference wasn't all that great.

Always, people had said of Carol that she was old for her years, even as a child, but then Ellen had tended to treat her as an adult before she was adult. She had taught Carol so much, would talk about anything and everything. Ellen's sister had been critical of this, saying that in the absence of a husband Ellen was bringing up her daughter too quickly. Maybe that was so. But Carol wouldn't change a thing. Carol's feet were planted firmly on the ground, and while she was nothing special to look at, she was not lacking in confidence. She was too tall, too slim, possessed of a very ordinary face with features which were too sharp ... but she had inner qualities which made up for all that. Good foundations, as Ellen had called them.

The summer during which Carol had just turned eighteen had been quite magical—for her and for her mother. By a fluke, or perhaps at the hand of some kindly fate, Ellen had won a holiday for two as a result of her entering a competition in a women's magazine. It was a fifteen-day cruise on a huge liner, and it had been difficult to tell which of them was more excited about it—Carol or Ellen. On board the ship Ellen had met Sam, an American high school teacher who had not, he had said, had a proper vacation in more than ten years.

Well, he had certainly made up for that. He had taken six months off work and had been on a world trip; the cruise was the last leg of his journey. Thinking back, Carol wondered how he had managed to do that, because Sam was by no means wealthy and a trip around the world must have cost a fortune. Sam must have used his savings. She remembered, too, the way she and her mother had liked him instantly, loving the stories he told of his travels. He was alone, and lonely, and the three of them had spent most of their time together—until Carol realised what was happening between her mother and the American!

Ellen had laughingly denied it at first, saying that mature people didn't fall *in love*, that at her age and Sam's age (he was eleven years older than Ellen) love was more inclined to grow as people simply got used to each other. What rubbish! They'd fallen, all right— clichéd head over clichéd heels.

There might, just might, have been a problem if Carol's future, her career, hadn't been so carefully mapped out. In the autumn, she was starting her course at a polytechnic where she was to train for her work in the social services. She had no desire to emigrate then, knowing precisely what she wanted to do with her life. She urged her mother to accept Sam's proposal of marriage, to think, for once, of her own happiness. It wasn't difficult; Ellen knew Carol was perfectly capable of looking after herself, though she was reluctant to leave her daughter.

They had flown to San Francisco in early August, with airticket s which were paid for by Sam. Carol spent a week with them, seeing them married on the day before she returned to England. Ten months later, Paul was born and, Ellen wrote in one of her frequent letters, the newlyweds' happiness was complete. Sam had never been married before; they hadn't even discussed the idea of children when Ellen learned she was pregnant. But Sam was over the moon about it . . .

Now, Carol pulled the blankets more closely around her, hardly able to breathe for the pain in her heart. She turned her face into the pillow, wanting to cry but unable to. After a while, she heard Sam's nephew running a bath and she shook, herself mentally. She must get up, get dressed. She wanted to go to the hospital and see Paul.

Sam's house was very ordinary. It had three bedrooms, and while there was a second toilet downstairs, there was only one bathroom. Carol got out of bed and unpacked the clothes she had so hastily flung into a suitcase. The effort tired her; there was no denying she was still weak. She had been off work with pneumonia for the past five weeks, including a week in hospital, and the doctor wouldn't let her go back for another ten days. Wearily, she sank back on to the bed as she waited for the bathroom. Quite apart from the necessary return to health, when would she be able to go back to work? There was no knowing how long Paul would remain in this dreadful coma . . . there was no knowing how long it would take to get things sorted out here ... there would be so many things, so many formalities to attend to.

Arturo would help, of course. How long would he stay around? He lived in California, but hundreds of miles south—on the outskirts of San Diego, if she remembered correctly, in a place called La .... something or other. According to Sam, Arturo was married to his work, to the clinic he ran. How long could he stay away from his responsibilities?

Tomorrow, she would make it her business to talk to the man. So far, she hadn't had a chance to do that. She hadn't even been able to think straight, what with the shock, the speed with which she had left England ...

Never, never would she forget Arturo's phone call. It had come at three o'clock in the morning, when she had been fast asleep. Calmly, and as gently as one could impart such news, he had told her of the accident. Ellen and Sam had taken Paul to the zoo, and the saddest thing was that Paul had asked his father if they might go by bus. To Paul, so used to going everywhere in his father's car, a trip on the bus was in itself a treat. After leaving the zoo the three of them had been standing at a bus stop together with a dozen other people when a lorry ploughed into them. It seemed that the vehicle's steering had gone and there was nothing in the world the driver could do to prevent the accident. As well as Ellen and Sam, five people were killed outright and the rest, including Paul and the driver, were injured. Paul had not regained consciousness since it happened.

'It could last for weeks, couldn't it?' Carol asked the question about Paul's condition as soon as she joined Arturo in the living room. He handed her a cup of coffee from the pot he had made and she accepted it gratefully. Gone was the dark, formal suit he had worn to the funeral. He was dressed very casually now, in faded denims and a dark blue shirt, the top three buttons of which were open.

'It won't.' He said it quietly, the deep voice confident. Carol looked at him quickly. 'What does that mean?'

'He'll come out of it soon. He'll be all right. I told you I've spoken to the doctor in charge. Now don't worry about Paul—I promise you he'll recover.'

They lapsed into silence, Carol cringing inwardly as she remembered how her little brother had looked when she had visited him the previous night, just a few hours after she had landed at San Francisco airport ... his gorgeous little face so badly bruised and cut. In her capacity as a social worker she had visited many sick people, many hospitals, but never before had she been so sickened, so frightened. But Paul was her own family. Her professional veneer, the hardness she had deliberately cultivated, the emotional detachment when dealing with other people's problems, all sorts of problems, hadn't helped one iota. How could she be detached when the victim in this case was her five-year-old brother? How was she going to tell him about his parents? It was a sickening prospect ...

'Carol?'

Startled, she looked up quickly. 'I'm sorry, what did you say?'

Arturo Kane thought for a moment before speaking. 'I'd rather you didn't come to the hospital. There's little point, after all. Paul will be none the wiser, and you saw him last night. You should rest—you look very pale.'

'I'm always pale,' she shrugged. 'That's natural for me.'

'Yes,' he smiled, 'I remember you joking and telling Sam you'd never get a suntan even if you lived on the Equator. But you're unnaturally white. Have you taken a look in the mirror today?'

'Leave me alone, will you?' Her voice was tinged with impatience and she instantly regretted the way it sounded. She had nothing whatever against Arturo Kane. About him she could hardly feel more neutral. 'I'm sorry,' she said softly.

Again he smiled, shrugged and said nothing. Again they lapsed into silence. On the two occasions she had met him before, it had been just like this. They had had little to say to one another apart from the usual enquiries and courtesies.

She had met Arturo at the wedding and then again two Christmases ago when Sam had sent money for a plane ticket and she had spent two weeks in San Francisco. Arturo had flown from San Diego to spend Christmas Eve and Christmas Day with Ellen and Sam—so Carol had had barely three days of his company until now. She could hardly say she knew the man, but she knew quite a lot about him. Sam had talked about his nephew so often and with such pride. Arturo had lived with his uncle from the age of eight until he left home to go to medical college. She knew that Arturo's father, Sam's brother, had died, but she knew nothing about his mother except that she was Mexican. And the Mexican in Arturo was very evident.

He wasn't merely deeply tanned, he was naturally olive-skinned and incredibly dark-haired. His hair was densely black, slightly wavy and thick, brushed straight back from his face. On meeting him, quite detachedly Carol had surveyed him, acknowledged his handsomeness as everyone else surely must. His eyes were as black as his hair, fringed with black lashes any woman would give her eye-teeth to own. He was the sort of man who looked as though he needed a shave just a few hours after he had had one, and he had what could only be described as presence—probably due to his height. He was six feet three if he was an inch, and broad with it. Broad and solid, with not an ounce of excess flesh on him.

Apart from all that Sam had told her about Arturo's clinic and his professional brilliance, she had observed for herself that he was a man of few words, a man very much on an even keel; calm, probably unshockable and unshakeable. If he was a sensitive and understanding man, as Sam said, then it didn't show. He seemed, to Carol, almost without emotion. She wasn't sure whether she liked that about him. She did, however, like the fact that he seemed oblivious of his physical attractiveness.

He had shown no emotion today—none at all. The thought pulled her up short. Neither had she—until she had passed out. But it had all been boiling under the surface from the moment she had got the phone call. She looked at Arturo as she sipped her second cup of coffee. It must be the same for him. Of course it must. And he had dealt with everything, the arrangements for the funeral, the identification . . .

In a sudden rush of gratitude towards him, she said, 'I'll make us a hot meal when we get back from the hospital, okay?'

His eyebrows rose slightly. 'That means you're ignoring my advice again? Coming to the hospital?'

'I——' She sighed inwardly. He didn't seem to understand. She couldn't *not* go to the hospital. 'Yes, of course I am.'

Stealthy in his movements, Arturo got to his feet, stretching. For such a big man he moved with a lot of grace. 'I'll get the car out. You wait here for the moment. Bring a jacket with you.'

'You didn't say . . . what about food? You must be starving.'

'You must be starving. You've eaten two biscuits and one sandwich since you set foot on American soil. I'll take you for a steak after we're through at the hospital.'

Carol put down her coffee cup, taken aback. It seemed that Dr Kane had been monitoring her food intake! He was a strange sort of man, she mused, and she never felt fully relaxed in his company.

In the middle of the night she made her way quietly downstairs and brewed a pot of tea. Her internal clock had been thrown out of gear by the time difference between England and California. Never before had she felt so physically exhausted, too exhausted to sleep. Until she could make at least an outline of a plan, she would never rest. She found a pad of paper and, typically, tried to set about it logically.

An hour later the paper was still blank. Money was the first problem, and even she, by nature an optimist, realised she would need some financial help in order to provide a reasonable life for Paul. After her mother's emigration, Carol had sold their small terraced house in Bolton and had bought a one-bedroomed flat there, in a better area. It was quite old, but it had cost more than she had got for the house. She wasn't particularly well paid, but the small mortgage she had taken on presented no problem. A two-bedroomed place, however, would cost more; she would really like a small house with a garden for Paul to play in. That would cost money, and there would be solicitor's fees, removal fees, extra furniture to buy . . .

She smiled, more from a sense of helplessness than anything else. She had no money! None at all. This year, a year which had started so beautifully, had managed to take up all her reserves, what with one thing and another. Ellen and Sam had brought Paul to England last Christmas. It had been Paul's first visit to his mother's homeland and he had been absolutely delighted to see his first snow. They had stayed at Ellen's sister's because it was too impractical to put them up in Carol's flat. They had all brought in the New Year at a party at which there had been over forty guests—and then, from the third of January onwards, when her family had gone back to the States, everything seemed to go wrong for Carol. Her car had been stolen, and while the insurance company had paid out, she had still spent some of her savings on finding a reliable replacement. Shortly after that her flat had needed rewiring, then she had had pneumonia, and now . . . this.

She shoved the pad and pencil to one side and made a fresh pot of tea. Something would turn up. It always did. She nodded to herself as if to affirm the thought, her optimism unshaken. Still, there were certain practicalities which had to be faced: she would have to get herself a desk job. At the moment she worked out in the field and her hours were by no means regular. It wasn't unheard of for her to be called out in the middle of the night to some crisis or other. That would be out of the question now Paul would be living with her. And her evenings helping to run the youth club would have to stop, too. She would have to talk to her boss; perhaps she could work in the administrative side of the services.

Seeing her first chink of light, she reached for the pad again and wrote: 'Sell the car and the V.T.R'. The car had been necessary for her job, and she had been paid an allowance for it. But if she could land a nine-to-five desk job, she could live without a car.

Her video tape recorder had been her one and only real indulgence. She was studying sociology and psychology with the Open University and had used the machine to record the programmes which were televised at unsocial hours. Well, once she had a regular job she would be able to get up early to watch them.

Laughing aloud, humourlessly, hollowly, Carol got to her feet. Who was she trying to kid? Distasteful though it seemed at this moment, she and Arturo would have to sort out her parents' finances and come up with some arrangement. On that note, she went to bed. Daylight had stolen slowly into the kitchen. It was a new day.

After a late breakfast, Arturo made a lengthy telephone call to his clinic and Carol went into Sam's study and typed a letter to her boss, explaining all that had happened. She didn't bother to phone, since she wasn't expected back at work yet in any case. She did telephone her aunt, though, who had been unable to attend Ellen's funeral partly for financial reasons but mainly because her daughter had just given birth to twins and her assistance was needed.

During the afternoon, Carol finally managed to sleep for a couple of hours while Arturo went through Sam's papers. She woke to the aroma of something delicious in the process of cooking and found, for the first time in days, that she actually had an appetite. Normally her appetite was enormous; she ate well—anything and everything—and never put on a pound. Actually, she wished she could. Especially now. On her, the weight loss she had undergone during her illness looked dreadful.

She examined herself in the bedroom mirror. She had lost about eight pounds and her ribs looked horribly protuberant. Her face was completely colourless and her hazel eyes, her one redeeming feature, looked washed-out now, too big for her face. Disgusted at her reflection, she turned away from the mirror and slipped into a pair of denims and a sweater. The jeans felt baggy on her and her breasts, more ample than one would expect on such a slim girl, nevertheless didn't fill her bra the way they had a few weeks ago. She never usually bothered about how she looked, and she wasn't interested in clothes, but she really must make an effort at least to regain the weight she had lost.

'That smells good,' Carol smiled as she walked into the kitchen to find Arturo basting a chicken. 'Have you sprinkled it with herbs or something?'

'Uh-huh.' He slipped the roasting tin back into the oven and straightened, the sheer size of him making the kitchen suddenly seem smaller. 'Coffee?'

'Let me make it.'

He waved her into a chair. 'It's made, can't you smell it?'

'No,' she smiled, 'I can only smell food.' The smile dropped from her face as she helped herself to cream and sugar. 'There's no word from the hospital yet . . .' It wasn't a question. She knew Arturo would have woken her if there had been any news.

'No. I——'

The telephone rang then, making Carol jump out of her skin, and she snatched up the receiver. It was Barbie, the neighbour, inviting her and Arturo to dinner. 'Thank you,' Carol's heart sank like a stone, 'but Arturo's in the middle of cooking right now. It was very kind of you, Barbie, we appreciate it . . . Yes, we're all right, thanks. Yes, I'm fine. Really.'

She hung up, meeting Arturo's eyes. 'I thought——'
'So did I.'

The waiting was awful. *Awful.*

'I . . . We have to talk, Arturo. About Paul. About
money. I know it seems—I mean, it's so soon, but
really——'

'It seems practical.' He put his own full-stop on her
attempted apology. 'And you're a practical girl, aren't
you?'

It was the first personal comment he had made about
her—to her face, at least. Unhesitatingly she agreed.
'Yes, very much so.'

He sat facing her, folding his arms across his broad
chest. 'Well, money presents no problem at all. So let
me relieve you of that worry straight away.'

Inwardly, Carol sagged with relief. She had no idea
that relief was written all over her face. 'I—I knew
nothing of Sam's personal business, you see. I mean,
insurance and so on. I know this house is rented, but
that's about all.' She shifted slightly, finding this
conversation distasteful but necessary. 'You've been
through his papers. What's the situation? And what
sort of compensation can we expect from the—the
accident?'

'Compensation?' Arturo seemed not to understand
the word. Perhaps they called it something different in
America?

'The driver of the lorry—his insurance company.
There must be——'

'No.' He shook his head firmly. He had not
misunderstood her. 'Carol, I haven't had a chance to
tell you—the man wasn't insured. He ran a one-man
business, his lorry was unroadworthy, and if he weren't
dead, he'd be in a lot of trouble with the police.'

'He—died?'

'After I called you, before you got here.'

'Did he have a family?'

'According to the police, he left three children.'

Carol looked away, feeling sick to her stomach and

angry at the world, the stupidity of some of the people in it.

When she didn't speak, Arturo said quietly, 'I entirely agree with you. Well, back to Sam. He had very little in savings. Sam was the type of man who spent his money as he went along, he'd always been like that. He was insured, but not for a great deal. You're aware that my uncle was somewhat eccentric—he'd never believed in life insurance, but he did something about that when he married Ellen. Still, there's the funeral and Paul's hospital bill——'

'Dear God!' Carol had completely forgotten about the absence of a National Health Service in America. The hospital bill alone could amount to a small fortune.

Arturo looked at her questioningly. After a slight pause he said, 'I spoke to the insurance company this afternoon.' He shrugged, telling her how much money they could expect from Sam's insurance, and it really wasn't what she'd hoped for.

Carol kept quiet. She wasn't going to let him see she was bothered by any of this. She knew she would cope—somehow. Nothing was said for a while, but Arturo was watching her closely. Then he added, 'Of course I shall pay the funeral and hospital bills.'

'There's no reason for you to do that,' she said firmly. 'We'll pay everything from the insurance.'

'There's every reason. I can afford it. I want to. Okay?'

He'd started by telling her money was no problem. To him, it wasn't. But it was different for her. She nodded in acceptance of his offer. Again they lapsed into silence while Arturo busied himself by dishing up the food and Carol laid the table. The meal was delicious. Arturo Kane was obviously a very capable man.

'Thank you.' She put her knife and fork together. 'That was good. I'll wash up before we go to the hospital.'

He went into the living room and left her to it.

There was no change in Paul. Carol and Arturo had words with the doctor in charge of his case, but she had the feeling that that was just for her benefit. It was only a question of waiting; Arturo knew that better than she. He had reassured her, and now Paul's doctor had personally reassured her.

'I want to thank you, Arturo,' she said as soon as they were back at Sam's house and settled with a cup of coffee.

He looked vaguely surprised. He was sitting in an armchair, his long legs stretched out before him, looking completely relaxed. 'For what?'

'For all you've done.'

'They're my relatives, too, Carol. What did you expect?'

She nodded, keeping quiet for a moment. 'About the money. How long will it be before things are sorted out? Did Sam actually leave a will?'

The dark eyes looked at her questioningly again. 'Yes. But things get a little complicated here, since Sam's beneficiary died too, and Paul's a minor. I'm seeing Sam's lawyer tomorrow afternoon, as a matter of fact.' He hooked a leg over the arm of his chair. His hand came up to rub the back of his neck as he added, 'Come with me by all means.'

Carol looked at him curiously. She had the feeling she was being scrutinised beyond the casual look he was giving her, felt that there was a question behind what he was saying. It was a little confusing and she felt ill at ease.

'And there are the cars,' he added. 'Sam's isn't worth much, but Ellen's is in pretty good shape. They hadn't finished paying for it, but it'll realise a few hundred dollars, I guess.'

She nodded. 'Then as soon as things are sorted out . . . By the way, how long can you stay in San Francisco?'

'What?'

'Obviously you want to see Paul on his feet, but—I mean, now long can you stay away from your clinic?'

'Greenacres isn't a clinic.' He waved a hand at the irrelevance of that remark. 'As long as necessary.' He swung his leg down and got to his feet. 'I think there's a bottle of brandy in the cupboard. Would you like a drink?'

'Very much, thanks.'

'I was about to ask you the same question. How long can you stay? What's happening with your job? I take it you still work in the social services?'

'Yes. There's no problem there. My doctor wouldn't let me go back to work for another ten days.'

'I'm glad to hear it——'

'And I've written to my boss. They'll have to expect me when they see me. As soon as Paul's well enough, we'll go. If things aren't sorted out here, then I'm sure you'll——'

Arturo was pouring their drinks and he turned to face her, his expression making her stop in mid-sentence. 'Go? Who'll go? Where?'

She looked at him blankly. 'To England, of course. As soon as Paul's fit to travel, I'll take him home.'

'What?' The word was barely audible. Arturo's dark eyebrows were pulled together as if she'd said something insulting or vulgar. 'Now just a minute——' The bite in his voice was so out of character that it shook her. 'Let's clear this up here and now! Paul stays with *me*! There is no way, and I mean *no way*, you're taking him out of this country!'

CHAPTER TWO

WITHOUT realising it, Carol got to her feet. She wasn't angry, she was absolutely dumbfounded. 'Paul stays with you? What are you talking about?'

His eyes glinted as he stared at her, as black as ebony and just as hard. 'I don't think I can put it more plainly.'

Carol's breath caught in an inaudible gasp. She became conscious of her heartbeat. They stood facing one another, their eyes locked together. In the pit of her stomach she felt something shift sickeningly . . . a sense of fear . . . panic. She returned his stare steadily, facing him squarely, knowing instinctively that she must assert herself as she had never needed to before. It was something she was good at, and it was vitally important she left no room for doubt in his mind. Not an inch. 'Forget it,' she said calmly, the impact of her words strengthened by the quietness of her voice.

In that way the mind has of thinking, or realising, several things all at the same time Carol saw that Arturo had taken for granted his guardianship of Paul just as much as she had. They had each done that to the extent that the subject, important as it was, hadn't even been mentioned until now. And they had each assumed the other's automatic compliance.

She knew also that Arturo Kane was thinking the same thoughts as she was, realising he must make his stand, stake his claim. The seconds ticked by. Informative seconds, seconds during which she knew that Arturo had suddenly become an adversary, that there was a lot of trouble in the air. For the moment they were battling in silence. One could have cut the atmosphere between them with a knife, so strong was the tension.

And she knew also that he was playing a game with

her—right now. Oh, it was a very grown-up game, a game of tactics, of psychological one-upmanship. But he couldn't know that she knew the rules, that she was by no means easily intimidated. And that was what he was trying to do. He was trying to gain an advantage, to intimidate her with his stance, his macho physique, his superior height, with the dark, arrogant look he was giving her. He was wasting his time! Paul was her brother!

Still, her heartbeat accelerated a little painfully.

'Thank you.' With a deliberate movement, Carol reached out and took the glass from his long fingers. She took a sip of the brandy and sat down. 'I suppose I'd better point out to you,' she said mildly, 'the impracticality of your *whim*.'

She knew instantly she'd made a big mistake. He actually flinched at the word she had used—used quite deliberately, of course. Beyond the depths of his tan, he paled slightly as pure rage tightened the muscles of his face, drawing his lips into a thin line. In that fleeting moment she caught a glimpse of something she would never have dreamt existed in him. His anger was so immense, so tangible that she felt as if he had struck her.

More than anything, she wanted to apologise. Not because she was afraid of him, but because she had insulted him dreadfully. She had used the word whim calculatingly, as a tactic against the force of his own determination, and it had backfired on her. And then some. She knew in that moment that she would get precisely nowhere if she tried anything like that again.

His anger had vanished now. It had gone as quickly as it had flared. But Carol had seen it, and it unnerved her. Oh, she hadn't thought for an instant that he would actually hit her. What unnerved her was her discovery that there was far more to Arturo Kane than met the eye. The calm personality had suddenly taken on new dimensions for her. The placid exterior hid ... what sort of man was he, actually?

She didn't apologise, because it wouldn't help her cause. Rather, she absorbed her new-found knowledge, filed it away and continued as if she had said nothing wrong. 'Arturo, I think you're acting impulsively, though it's very understandable. Paul is now an orphan. You're his only relative in the entire U.S.A. But he has a ready-made home with me in England, and there are several other relatives of his there. . . .'

As he turned his back on her, she faltered. He drank his brandy straight off, put the glass on the windowsill and just stood, looking out at the street.

'. . . You've got to look at it from a practical point of view, Arturo. It's obvious that Paul must come to me.'

Beneath the dark material of his shirt, she saw the muscles of his shoulders relax. He was smiling when he turned to face her, but she didn't like it one little bit. He nodded shortly, as if he had made up his mind about something.

In some distant corner of her mind, beyond her unhappiness and all the arguments she had ready for this battle, something shifted. What had hitherto been a feeling of complete neutrality towards Arturo Kane had changed to a feeling of intrigue. It was too nebulous, too unimportant to examine more closely now; there was too much at stake to risk losing her concentration.

'I must make allowances for you,' he said quietly. 'I must make allowances and put all you've said down to the fact that you're distraught. You've had a tremendous shock, which even now you haven't fully absorbed, and you're physically unwell. You didn't sleep at all last night, or the night before, and you snatched only two restless hours this afternoon.'

She looked at him sharply. How did he know about this afternoon? Had he stood outside her door and listened or something?

'You were calling out in your sleep,' he said. 'Calling for your mother.'

Shocked, Carol looked down at the carpet. She felt humiliated. If she had heard someone else doing what she had done, she would have understood it and sympathised. But because she had done it, she felt humiliated. Anger flared up in her, anger towards Arturo, but she clamped down on it because it was illogical, unfair. Why should she be angry with him just because he had told her something about herself she'd rather not have known?

'This is a very emotional time for you,' he went on, 'I appreciate that. You're distraught and you're physically exhausted. The mind and the body are a team, Carol. They work hand in hand, each acting upon the other. You're so tired, you can hardly walk straight, so——'

'Save it!' she snapped. 'If you're about to tell me I'm so upset that I can hardly *think* straight, don't bother!' She was fuming, all attempts at keeping her anger in check were abandoned. Who the hell did he think he was talking to?

'Don't talk to me as if I were one of your patients!' she shouted. She made a sound of pure frustration in the back of her throat. More quietly, she added, 'You're not the first psychiatrist I've known. I've met several in the course of my work and they all seem to think that what they say is gospel! One of them is as daft as a brush ...'

She saw the corners of his lips twitch and she glared at him. 'In other words, I'm not impressed! Yes, I'm upset. Yes, I'm tired. But don't try to undermine my common sense by speaking like the venerable authority and telling me I'm distraught!' Realising that she in fact sounded distraught, she calmed herself quickly. 'We've moved away from the point of this conversation. Paul is coming to England with me. He's my brother. He's five years old and he needs a mother. You may visit him any time you wish.'

Arturo's broad shoulders lifted in a shrug. He sat down, flung his leg over the side of the chair again and shook his head as if he didn't know what to do with her. 'You didn't listen properly, did you? I was trying to explain that you're as tired mentally as you are physically. What I mean is that everything will seem different to you in a few days' time. You'll see things as they really are.' Calmly, patiently, he asked, 'Do you really think I'm the sort of man who would act on a whim? Granted, you don't know me—but do you really think that?'

'No,' she said simply, honestly.

'Then why say it?'

'It was my way of scorning the idea that you should have Paul. I wanted to put you down because you tried to intimidate me. You're still trying to. And I wanted to make you see you were acting on impulse, instead of common sense. But you've turned the tables on me and now you're trying to convince me I'm acting from emotion.'

Arturo's eyebrows rose and he bowed his head slightly as if she had impressed him. 'Thanks for your honesty. I'd come to the conclusion that you were trying to put me down.' He smiled, and still she didn't like it. She found she was bracing herself for whatever he was going to say next.

'So,' he said slowly, 'you're honest as well as practical.'

She said nothing. Some intuition told her she was getting nowhere, in spite of his compliments. There was trouble in the wind; she could almost smell it. A pulse in her temple started throbbing. 'So where do we go from here?'

'A boy needs a father-figure, Carol. I know that from my own experience.'

'A child needs a mother, Arturo. I know *that* from my own experience.'

They looked at each other. No score. Still no score.

When he smiled then it was very different because it was genuine, humorous. It prevented any nastiness forming between them. 'Ellen brought you up single-handed, didn't she?'

'And Sam took you under his wing when you were eight.'

Thoughtfully, he said, 'Paul's an extremely bright

little fellow, did you know that? Did you know he has an advanced reading age?'

'Yes, I did.'

'How much of his potential is realised will depend on so many things: his home life, his personal security, his environment, the education he receives. Now, Carol, what can you offer the boy?'

She knew a slight sense of defeat. Arturo was waving his money at her, and she couldn't match that. 'Love,' she said softly. 'All that he needs. It's something you didn't mention just now.'

'Ah, yes ... love.' He sighed. It was a very weary sound. 'Love can be so many things. It's often more negative than positive. It can mean emotional slavery. It can crush. It can smother. It can make one act illogically and, as in your case now, it can be extremely selfish.'

Carol opened her mouth to speak and promptly closed it again. The trouble was that while she had never, ever, thought of love in those terms, she could see what he meant. She blinked at the thought; there was a lot of truth in what he had said. 'Explain. About me, I mean.'

'You were thinking of uprooting Paul and taking him to live in the industrial north of England, where the climate is cold and damp. Taking him to a foreign country where the educational system is inferior to ours, where the summers are sparse and the standard of living is lower. Worse, you were forgetting the trauma he's yet to face through the loss of both parents simultaneously, and you'd add to that trauma by taking him away from his native country, from all that's familiar and safe to him. To a place where he would be pointed at by other children because he speaks differently, where he would have to make yet another adjustment. Where he would have to learn—well, almost a new language, a new culture.'

The silence hung in the air between them. Carol didn't know what to say. There was so much she wanted to say! 'I—I think you're being——' She floundered. Damn it all, the way he'd painted the picture made it sound as if she'd be doing something dreadful!

'My last remark ...' he grinned. 'It was a slight exaggeration—to make the point.'

'Yes, yes,' she waved her hand impatiently. It had been quite a speech, coming from him. Score one. Maybe even two. Frustration alone was preventing her from replying. She was short of an answer—and she was never short of an answer! He was so damn clever— he'd fazed her completely.

'In case you've forgotten my original statement,' he said drily, 'I'd begun by pointing out to you how selfish love can be.'

'I haven't forgotten!' she snapped. She got to her feet and helped herself to another drink, her hands trembling as she held the bottle.

When a minute had passed and she still hadn't answered him, he said, 'I see you're quick to learn, too. That's something else I've discovered about you. You've realised there's no point in our continuing this conversation, that that little American citizen is going to stay where he belongs—where he's much better off.'

'Damn it, are you still talking in terms of money and education?' she blurted. 'And while we're on that subject—what you said about our educational system was purely a matter of opinion. And what would you know about it? Why do you suppose young people from all the corners of the world are sent to England to be educated!'

'Because it's the "thing" to do?' he offered. 'Because the "British education" still lives on its former glory?'

Very calmly, very coldly, she said, 'You won't win, Arturo.'

He grimaced. 'Win?'

She looked down at the amber liquid in her glass. 'Yes, I know that sounds awful. But I can't think of a better word.'

'Come to think of it, neither can I.'

'So. We've reached deadlock.' Carol sipped at her drink and sat down tiredly, her hand reaching up to rub her throbbing temple. 'Because I'm not impressed by anything you've said to me. I take your point, that love can sometimes be selfish. But it isn't in this case, in my case. It certainly wouldn't be in Paul's best interests to hand him over to you!'

Some of that was true, some of it wasn't. Arturo was married to his work. He lived on the premises of Greenacres, his clinic or whatever he called it and, according to Sam, used his apartment only to sleep in. He was totally committed, dedicated. Where would a five-year-old fit into his life?

On the other hand, California was a nice place to live, with its temperate climate, high standard of living . . . she had thought of going to live there herself, with Ellen and Sam. They had all discussed it at considerable length, in fact. But that was academic now. And Paul would make the necessary adjustment to living in England. Of course he would! The fact that he was only five was a good thing. It would have been harder if he'd been, say, fourteen, and had a lot of friends, perhaps a girl-friend . . .

Carol pulled herself up short. What was she doing, even thinking these thoughts? There was no question of her handing Paul over to Arturo!

'How bad is it?' he asked suddenly.

'What?'

'Your headache, of course.'

'I haven't . . . fairly bad.' She didn't have the energy to lie. Why bother, anyhow?

He got up and came over to her, pulling her gently to her feet and keeping hold of her. 'I'm sorry.'

'For what?' She raised her eyes to his, trying to shrug his hand from her arm.

'This scene, at this particular time—when all you want is to cry.' He paused. 'But perhaps it's as well that you get used to things from the start. Reality, I mean.

The reality that Paul is coming to live with me.' His hand tightened on her arm, uncomfortably so.

'Don't do that, Arturo.' Her voice was like ice. 'I'm not easily intimidated—even by a big man.'

Almost sadly, he smiled at her. 'How little you know me! But then that's just one of the problems between us. If I were trying to intimidate you . . . Carol, I'm holding on to you because you're swaying on your feet. And we both know what happened the last time you did that. Would you like a sleeping tablet?'

'No, thank you.'

'Are you likely to sleep tonight, without one?'

'I'm sure of it,' she lied.

Luckily, she did sleep that night. It was hardly surprising, considering how short of sleep she was. Yet she had gone to bed with her mind in such a turmoil she had felt sure she would end up drinking tea again in the early hours.

Arturo was right about one thing: everything did seem different to her now she was rested. She got up at noon, having slept solidly for thirteen hours. She didn't look any better, but she certainly felt it.

Wearing yesterday's denims and a plain white blouse, Carol went downstairs. It was warmer today. In a few days' time it would be May. The noon sun was streaming through the windows and there wasn't a hint of the mist which so often hung around this part of the State. On the kitchen table was a note from Arturo, saying he had gone to see Sam's lawyer, that he had thought it more important for her to sleep than to go with him. She shrugged on reading it, suddenly realising why Arturo had looked at her strangely when she had been asking him about Sam's finances. Since he had taken it for granted he was going to look after Paul, he must have thought she had been asking about the money for herself. Yuk! What must he have thought of her then? Oh, they'd certainly been at cross purposes!

But never mind. Whatever he had thought of her during these past few days had been revised—several times! She had told him, shown him, that she wouldn't be bullied or intimidated. She'd made him see she was by no means a fool, but a thinker.

She put the kettle on and sat at the table, waiting, her fingers strumming lightly against its surface. She might have asserted herself with Arturo Kane, but she still hadn't solved the problem. No conclusion had been reached. He was still as determined to have Paul as she was. And that sense of trouble still hung ominously in the air.

The telephone rang, and again Carol almost jumped out of her skin. It was Uncle George, Ellen's brother-in-law.

'Hello, love. Just ringing to see how you are.'

The familiar, kindly voice made her feel better. 'I'm okay, Uncle George. How's everyone at that end? The new twins . . .? Has Aunty Jean come home yet, or is she still acting as nursemaid?'

They kept it brief because transatlantic phone calls are expensive, but naturally her uncle asked about Paul, his health, and Carol told him in no uncertain terms that she would be bringing the boy home as soon as he was fit to travel. She smiled to herself when her uncle said he had taken that much for granted.

Why couldn't Arturo see the sense in it, too?

She took her tea into the back garden—or the back yard, as Americans called it—and sat, thinking about Arturo. When she closed her eyes, she found she could see his face as clearly as if he were there, but then it was a striking face. She examined it mentally, thinking it a pity she had never done this before. If she had taken the trouble to look closely when she had met him on the two previous occasions, she might have been forewarned about his hidden depths.

But she had never looked beyond the handsomeness of his face in its entirety. While she was by no means inclined to romanticise, she had thought his eyes beautiful in their unusual blackness, their frame of thick lashes. Pity she had never noticed how intense they were, how watchful. And that was a no-nonsense chin, square, determined. Perhaps it was the strong, clearly-defined jawline which added a touch of arrogance? Or was it the nose, which could be called neither straight nor hooked? Well, if anything maybe very slightly hooked. If she hadn't known he was thirty-six, she would have had trouble guessing his age within, say, a ten-year span. He could have been thirty, he could have been forty.

When the lines of his forehead and those at the side of the nose and mouth deepened with age he would still be handsome. At the moment they spoke of character and, no doubt, his own share of worry. In fact the whole face spoke of character, especially in the eyebrows—always an indicator of character—thick, nicely-shaped and as black as his hair.

Carol put her cup on the grass and lay back on the sun-lounger, relaxing under the warmth of the sun. Arturo wasn't remotely like his uncle, who'd been blond, but then he was half Mexican. His darkness made him seem mysterious to her now ...

How stupid! she chided herself. It had nothing to do with his darkness! He had become mysterious because he was an unknown quantity. Even his voice was dark—deep. Though he was quietly spoken. She'd never heard him raise his voice, yet he had managed to take her breath away with his vehemence when last night's argument had begun. And he spoke, always, as if what he was saying could not be argued with.

Carol decided he was arrogant.

He was a very 'together' person. Another Americanism, and what a good word it was! She liked to think of herself as being together—self-sufficient, capable, with inner strength. Arturo could be leaned on, as she could. In fact he probably thrived on that—look at the profession he'd chosen.

She decided she liked him in spite of his arrogance.

It was his anger, that intense anger she had seen stamped on his features for such a fleeting moment, which had triggered this analysis. She reminded herself of that. It was because of that that she had suddenly become interested in Arturo Kane. If interested was the right word. Intrigued was probably a better word. She knew, though she couldn't say why she knew, that his anger would never be given vent to. He was too controlled. His anger, like his other emotions, was very tightly harnessed.

She decided she envied his self-control.

He had behaved, coped, far better last night than she had. First, she had openly insulted him, then she had lost her temper twice. Her lack of control annoyed her in itself. And she had let herself down in more ways than one: hadn't she been trying to make Arturo see she was a fit and capable guardian for Paul—a better guardian than he would be? She thought again of all he had said about love, the negative side of it. Then his blunt statement that her love for Paul was making her behave selfishly.

Was there any truth in that? Carol never dismissed new ideas without thinking them over. Her job had taught her a lot about human nature, but she didn't pretend to know it all. Would it be selfish of her to take Paul to England? Did she want him for her own sake instead of wanting what was best for him?

Of course she wanted him for her own sake. And so what? She loved him and she wanted him with her. But there was nothing selfish about that! Telling Paul this, that he was loved and wanted, would at least help a little in making up for the boy's loss. And she knew without doubt that her mother would have wanted her to have Paul, rather than Arturo having him. So would Sam, come to think of it. He had often bemoaned the fact that Arturo spent twenty hours of his day working.

Carol closed her eyes against the glare of the sun. She would make one more attempt to make Arturo see sense. And if he didn't agree to her wishes—well, she would simply have to pull rank on him—point out to him that he really had no choice in the matter.

She slept lightly, so lightly that when the sun was suddenly obscured by shadow, her eyes came open quickly. She looked up into the dark, fathomless eyes of a strikingly handsome face, saw the flash of strong and perfect teeth as the firm mouth parted in a smile. Inside her, very deep inside her, there came a sense of unease so strong that it seemed physical. It was disconcerting. Carol got quickly to her feet, feeling she was somehow at a disadvantage lying there like that . . . in the shadow of Arturo Kane.

CHAPTER THREE

'WHAT are you doing out here, in the cold?'

She avoided his eyes, laughing to hide her unease. 'It's funny what you Californians think of as cold. In England this would be counted as a summer's day. It's beautifully warm.' She walked ahead of him into the house. 'You must be ready for a cup of coffee.'

They had coffee in the living room, an awkward silence hanging between them. 'How—how did you get on at the lawyer's?'

'Fine.' Arturo gave a satisfied nod. 'He's sorting everything out. It's just a question of time. I left all Sam's papers with him.' He paused, and Carol could almost see his mind ticking over. She was getting used to the way he thought before he spoke. 'Carol, I've had an idea, a very constructive idea.'

'Yes?' She was prepared to listen. More than once she had been accused of stubborness, by her mum as well as by other people, but never let it be said she had a closed mind . . .

But the doorbell rang and Barbie Howard came in carrying something which smelled delicious. 'I've been cooking today,' she smiled. 'I've made pizzas.' She thrust a cardboard box into Carol's hands. 'I thought you might like a couple, you and Art. If you don't want them now, you can heat them up later.'

'Oh, Barbie, that's very kind of you. Thanks. I don't know about Arturo, but I'm certainly going to eat mine now.' She went through to the kitchen, realising she'd forgotten to eat anything that day.

'There's no news? From the hospital?' Barbie put the pizzas on the plates Carol handed to her.

Carol shook her head, swallowing against the lump in her throat. 'I'll tell Arturo——'

But he was already there, standing in the doorway and giving the neighbour an appreciative smile. Barbie helped herself to coffee and they ate, listening to her small talk. Again she offered her help, if there was anything she could do, as several other people had offered.

She stayed an hour, and by the time she left it was getting late and Arturo wanted to take a shower before they went to the hospital. Carol washed the dishes while she waited for him, ran a comb through her hair and clipped it into place at the nape, as usual. The hall mirror showed her that her hours in the sun had been worthwhile. She had some colour in her face, not that there was much at the best of times. She was hardly rosy-cheeked, but at least she no longer looked as white as a sheet. Her eyes looked a little more lively, too. They were still too big for her face, but at least they no longer looked washed out.

They were using Ellen's car. Arturo had left his own at San Diego airport and had flown to San Francisco, he'd said. Carol glanced at him several times during the short drive to the hospital, but nothing was said. Her thoughts were with Paul—until she found herself looking at Arturo's hands on the steering wheel. Big hands. Very brown with long fingers and immaculate nails which were kept short. They were strong, capable hands—a doctor's hands. She found herself wondering why he had gone on to specialise in psychiatry . . .

The low heels of her shoes clicked hollowly as they walked down the hospital corridor to Paul's room. Carol became conscious of the sound, feeling and knowing it was foolish, that it was somehow irreverent to make such a noise in that hushed atmosphere. Her stomach turned over nervously and the clicking ceased as she stopped abruptly in her tracks.

A doctor was stepping out of Paul's room, and in the moment it took for him to close the door, Carol heard the little boy crying for all he was worth. Unthinkingly she grabbed Arturo's arm as the doctor came towards them, his expression sombre.

And then he smiled. 'Dr Kane, Miss Palmer—if I might have a word. . . .'

They stepped into his office further down the corridor, and Arturo motioned Carol into a chair. 'When did he come out of it?'

'About an hour ago.' The doctor's smile broadened. 'It's all been pretty straightforward, Dr Kane. Paul will be just fine.' His smile faded somewhat as he added, still addressing Arturo, 'We'll keep him with us a few more days, but for the moment . . . he's asking for his parents.'

Crying for his parents, Carol corrected him mentally. What on earth would they tell him? *How* could they explain? The sound of the doctors' voices faded as she tried to take hold of herself. She had cultivated a hardness, a veneer which it was necessary to stand behind for much of the time in her job as a social worker. If she were not detached, if she allowed herself to get emotionally involved, it would detract from her efficiency. She'd coped with many people's crises, all sorts of crises, but this was her *own*; she *was* emotionally involved. . . .

'Would you rather stay here, Carol? Come in later, perhaps?'

She looked up to find that the doctor had gone, and Arturo was looking down at her, tall, erect, as composed as ever. 'No, I wouldn't! I can cope with my own dirty work, thank you!' She got smartly to her feet and walked out of the office.

'Just a minute.' The hand on her arm was like a vice. Arturo pulled her back into the doorway of the office. 'You can't go in looking like that. You look terrified.'

'I'm all right, I——'

'It's written all over your face, it's in your eyes. You're going to frighten the child.'

'I'll be perfectly all right.' She took a deep breath to steady herself. 'Really, I'll——' What followed was the last thing on earth she expected. If Arturo had slapped her, she couldn't have been more surprised.

But he didn't slap her. He kissed her. He pulled her towards him and locked his arms around her back, stopping her words with a kiss which left her breathless. As he raised his head she stared at him stupidly, thinking he'd lost his senses. She didn't know whether to laugh, cry or slap him. As realisation dawned, he kissed her again, and this time she struggled against him—to no avail.

He was trying to distract her, she realised, to chase the fear from her eyes before she went in to see Paul. How very clever of him! But he needn't bother! Her struggles increased and his arms tightened around her almost painfully as the kiss deepened. She was vaguely aware of people moving in the corridor, of the flash of white as they walked past the door. She heard a soft chuckle, a female sound, and then she was aware of nothing but the suddenly intimate turn the kiss had taken. Arturo's lips were exploring her mouth, demanding a response, and the space between their bodies had closed.

Carol relaxed against him, it was partly from lack of choice and partly deliberate because she realised that until he had achieved his objective, he would keep on kissing her . . . and that was a disturbing prospect.

At last he let go of her, and she took an involuntary step away from him, dumbstruck.

'Now you look angry.' His shrug was exaggerated in an attitude of helplessness. Helplessness! Then he grinned, and in spite of everything Carol heard herself laughing rather confusedly.

'Ready to go in?' he asked quietly.

'Ready.' She had levelled off emotionally, was no longer terrified and no longer angry. The kiss had been meaningless but purposeful and she thought no more about it. Not then, and not for a long time afterwards.

When they finally left the hospital, Carol was utterly

drained. Never in her life had she felt so empty, useless.
Yet never before had she been needed as she was
needed now. How Paul had sobbed—clinging to her
and begging her not to go away! Over and over again
he had asked the same question: 'Aren't they ever
coming back? Not *ever*?'

They drove in silence and she turned her face to the
window, looking at the streets of San Francisco
through a light haze of rain and a haze of tears which
she fought to keep under control. People, lights, traffic
flashed past her eyes and everything was slightly
distorted and seemingly moving in slow motion.

They had told Paul nothing constructive and he had
been too distressed to ask what was going to happen to
him. They had said everything possible in an effort to
comfort and console, but the boy had been inconsolable.
They had stayed until he had sobbed himself to sleep,
until the nurse had ushered them from the room.

Carol shuddered, hearing his repeated question
echoing round her head. Tomorrow he would surely
ask, 'Where will I live?' Her lips clamped together and
she looked at Arturo as he drove, feeling hatred
towards him, a hatred so strong that it almost choked
her. It was irrational, unfair, she knew that even as she
felt it. Oh, but nothing, *no one*, was going to take Paul
from her!

'You said earlier that you'd had a constructive idea,'
Carol said as soon as they had got past the front door
of the house. 'I'd like to hear it.'

Her voice was snappy, taut, and he shot her a quick
look as he walked straight through to the kitchen. 'I'll
make some coffee. You go and sit down. We'll talk
then.'

She did as he said, staring unseeingly around the
living room. When Arturo put the tray beside her, she
poured the coffee from the percolator automatically,
her hands trembling so that she spilled drops of the
scalding liquid over the side of the cups. 'Well?'

'Ellen and Sam spent a weekend with me in

February, as you may or may not know. They said that while they were in England over Christmas, you'd all discussed your possible emigration.'

'So?' She was trying not to be curt, but she wanted him to get quickly to the point.

'So why not emigrate? It would solve a lot of problems over Paul.'

'It isn't that easy—now,' she snapped. 'To get a job as a social worker here I'd have to train all over again—well, almost. The system's very different here, you know.'

'I'm aware of that. So what's the problem?'

The problem was money, of course. Sam and Ellen had wanted her to emigrate, had wanted her to live with them while she underwent her training. They would have been happy to keep her until she had got established. But they had all done nothing more than speculate on the matter, and when Carol had mentioned the idea to a colleague of hers she had been told to forget it; the U.S.A. did not hand out work permits readily—certainly not to foreigners who wanted to do a job which could easily be done by an American.

She said all of this to Arturo and he considered before he answered. 'I could probably pull a few strings—if you were willing to train.'

'And how would I live and pay rent during that time?' Even if she sold her flat, she couldn't manage. 'Forget it. It's impractical now.'

'Have you no funds at all, Carol?'

'No.' She didn't tell him she would even have to borrow the money for Paul's ticket to England. But her bank would lend her that much, she knew.

'That's a pity,' Arturo drawled. 'Because San Diego is a nice place to live, and if you'd moved there you could have had access to Paul any time you liked.'

What? She glared at him in disbelief. And he looked back at her as if he were wondering what was wrong. She got to her feet, moving around the room in sheer frustration. Was he just plain stupid or was he winding her up deliberately? All that talk about emigration—for what? Even if it were possible, for what? So Paul could live with *him!*

She halted by his chair, standing just two feet away from him and trying to count to ten before she spoke. She got to four. 'Clever, aren't you? Well, go to hell, Dr Kane! Go to hell!'

Arturo's arm shot out and his hand closed tightly around her wrist. 'Sit down, Carol.'

'Don't try——'

'Sit down.' His eyes closed briefly and his expression was shuttered, his face telling her only of his grim determination.

She sat. There was no visible evidence of his anger this time, but she knew it was there.

With a patience which was sickeningly patronising, he said, 'Since you obviously haven't changed your mind about Paul, I'll have to appeal to the practical side of your nature. You're a sensible girl, I'm sure you'll see things my way——'

She wanted to hit him, but she made no attempt to try it, because if this man ever did give vent to his emotions, she wouldn't like to be around when it happened. 'If you have any more so-called constructive ideas you know what you can do with them!'

'Now that isn't very ladylike, is it?'

'I've never professed to be a lady. I can put it far more bluntly, believe me.'

His tongue made a clicking sound. 'Carol, when we see Paul tomorrow, we have to tell him what's going to happen. We have to tell him where he's going to live, and with whom. And we both have to look happy about it—both of us.'

Carol put her hands to her face, slumping forward in the chair and resting her elbows on her knees. Her hands felt unusually cold, yet her face was unusually hot. Neither of them could offer Paul an ideal home life, she knew that. But of them both, she could offer him more. 'According to Sam, you're married to your job, you work all the hours God sends and have no time for——'

'An exaggeration,' he cut in. 'And I've been told something similar about you, by the way. That between your work and the time you spend helping to run a youth club, you have very little social life.'

'That is my social life—was my social life,' she amended. 'Look, if you want to sort this out, stop interrupting and listen to me. I will not have Paul brought up in a place where there are mentally disturbed people roaming around——'

'Don't be ridiculous! Greenacres is a halfway house for people who've been undergoing treatment but who are not yet ready to face the world again. By the time they get to Greenacres they're well on the way to recovery. And Paul would never see my patients. My apartment is completely self-contained.'

'And who'd look after him while you're at work? Who'd cook for him and put him to bed?'

'A housekeeper, of course. I'll hire someone who——'

'Who wouldn't give a damn!' she shouted. 'Someone who'd be working solely for the money and wouldn't really give a damn!'

'And you could offer something better?' he asked quietly. 'You can afford someone to look after him? Someone who'd really care? Or perhaps you're thinking of giving up work?'

There was no answer to that, of course. For a moment, Carol was plunged back into the past. Her mother had had to work full-time, had had to pay child-minders to look after Carol in the early years. Then, when she was older, she had been given a key which she wore on a piece of string around her neck so she wouldn't lose it. After school, she would let herself into the house and while away the time until Ellen got home. Sometimes her friends would be with her, and sometimes they weren't. Then it was lonely, without a brother or a sister to keep her company, even to fight with. In the winter it was already dark at four o'clock, and scary waiting in the——

Good grief, what was the matter with her? Not for years had she thought of this, the negative side of things. She stopped the train of thought instantly. There had been many advantages, too. The closeness with her mother for one thing, the self-sufficiency she had learned at an early age. Wasn't she, Carol, the living proof that an upbringing such as that need not affect one adversely? As long as there was love——

She got to her feet. The argument was over as far as she was concerned. She had tried to make Arturo see sense, and she had failed. Now it was time to pull rank. 'I'm going to bed, Arturo. I'm not willing to discuss the matter further. I've tried to be reasonable with you because your motives are good. But you see, you really have no choice in the matter. Paul is my brother. I'm taking him home to Bolton. And there's nothing you or anyone else can do to stop me.'

She got as far as the door before he spoke. 'Wait.'

There was such a flatness, almost a sadness, in his voice that it stopped her in her tracks. She turned to look at him, frowning. She could see the tension which had crept into his body, the muscle working in his jaw, and when he spoke, she had to strain to hear what he said. 'You don't understand, Carol. You couldn't begin to understand. Looking after Paul is something I have to do. I'm not prepared to explain my reasons. Just accept what I tell you, please.'

'I'm sorry,' she said softly. She was, too. Truly sorry, because something about his tone had touched her deeply and she understood what he meant. His reasons didn't matter. The trouble was that she felt exactly the same. 'I do understand, Arturo. But it makes no difference.'

'Wait.'

This time Carol felt her hand tightening on the door handle. He had stopped her with the same, solitary word, spoken at the same pitch, but his voice was as cold as ice now and her stomach contracted nervously. She felt threatened.

'You're wrong, Carol. You can be stopped from taking Paul. He isn't your brother, he's your half-brother. Bear in mind that I spoke to Sam's lawyer this afternoon. As Paul's cousin, I have as much right to claim guardianship of Paul as you have.'

Carol felt the blood draining from her face. 'Are you . . . are you threatening me with a legal battle?'

Very quietly, he asked, 'Can't you afford a legal battle?'

'You *bastard*!' She hadn't even thought about money, she'd been too shocked, disgusted, at the notion of fighting it out in the courts. 'Good God, man,' she shouted, 'think what that would do to Paul! Think! Oh, it's just what he needs right now, isn't it? To be dragged through the courts, the centre of a legal battle between his two loving relations! It's obscene, Arturo! How can you even consider it? You, more than anyone, should realise the effect that could have on him!'

'Then stop fighting me now,' he shrugged.

'I don't believe you're serious!' He was bluffing. Surely he was bluffing? Of course he was aware how badly Paul could be affected by such action! Especially now!

Arturo got slowly to his feet and came over to where she was standing. His face, his eyes, his voice were completely devoid of emotion. 'Oh, yes, I'm serious.'

She looked away from him, unable to stand the coldness of his eyes.

'Furthermore,' he said, 'I would win. There's that unavoidable word again. Consider it, Carol; an American child, American courts, a respected doctor who can offer far more——'

She swore. In no uncertain terms she told him what to do with himself, but it had no effect whatsoever. Again he shrugged. 'That kind of talk will get us nowhere. The choice is yours, unless you can come up with something constructive yourself. You've got about twenty hours before we visit the hospital. So unless you can come up with a better idea, you can give me your decision over whether we go to court or not in the morning. Goodnight, Carol.'

Carol would never, she thought, forget these days in San Francisco. And how many more were there yet to face? What was she going to do? Throughout the night she asked herself that question over and over again. But first, she cried.

As soon as her bedroom door was closed behind her, she sobbed as she had never sobbed before. The dam broke and all the pent-up emotions of the past few days came pouring out. She didn't even get undressed. For more than an hour she cried herself wretched and then lay, exhausted, on top of the bedclothes.

She felt a perverse pleasure on hearing Arturo moving around in the middle of the night. Were her tears keeping him awake? Or was he having an attack of conscience? Did he have a conscience? Whatever, she was glad he couldn't sleep.

He would win, of course. A disgusting word in this context, for no matter who won, Paul would lose. An irrelevant thought—irrelevant. Because there was no way she was going to court. She would not call Arturo's bluff. That man was capable of anything.

Her mind went round in circles. Paul had clung to Arturo as much as he had clung to her. He'd called him 'Uncle Art . . .' but they were cousins, in fact, the blond boy and the dark-haired man. The dark-haired man. The bastard! She thumped her pillow viciously, feeling trapped, frustrated, defeated.

The hell she was defeated! She'd come up with something. But what? The trouble was that deep inside she was too soft. Beneath that tough veneer there was too much compassion, too much understanding. That was why she had chosen a career of helping other people, trying to solve their problems. There were times, of course, when she let her compassion show. Times when that was the right, the only thing to do.

So she couldn't hate Arturo. How could she, when he seemed to feel a need as strong as her own? The realisation made her anger dissipate. Oh, but he was a strange mixture of a man . . .

Irrelevant, irrelevant. *What* was she going to do?

Time and again her mind strayed away from that question and she forced it back again. There was one solution, of course. But it was too preposterous even to suggest. Arturo would laugh himself silly. If he were capable of actually laughing . . .

With the first hint of daybreak there was the sound of a car engine being started—someone going off to work early. Then a dog started yapping furiously. A front door slammed shut and the barking stopped. The new day had started. The light filtered through the beige material of the curtains.

Carol turned over and caught sight of herself in the mirrored door of the wardrobes which were built into the wall on the left of the bed. What a badly thought-out room. She didn't care to look in the mirror first thing in the morning. Especially this morning, when her eyes were swollen and red.

She got up. Her thinking could take her no further than it had, no matter how long she lay there. It was six in the morning. Arturo was in the kitchen; she could hear him moving around, as he'd moved around all night. She got into the bathroom before he wanted it, showered, bathed her eyes and put on fresh clothes.

Then she went downstairs because she had made up her mind about what to say. Her mind was clear now and she was certain, almost certain, that she'd walked into some sort of trap the night before. Arturo had been bluffing about going to court. She was sure of it— almost. Well, she'd see. She would call his bluff in return. Two could play at that game!

Or was her preposterous idea her last, her only solution?

'Good morning, Carol.'

'Good morning.' She sat at the kitchen table and accepted his offer to make tea for her. He had learned by now that she never drank coffee first thing in the morning.

How very civilised this was! How very civilised, she mused, their behaviour, when they were both fiercely resenting one another. Her eyes were still puffy from weeping, but her facial expression was one of composure and it hid, she hoped, the nervousness churning inside her. If she had made a mistake about Arturo, if her own bluff didn't work, then she would be left with no choice but to try and talk him into her alternative solution.

He asked the question as he handed her her tea. 'Have you reached a decision yet, or do you need a few more hours to think about it?'

'I've made up my mind,' she said, meeting his eyes. 'We'll go to court and let them decide.'

When she saw the surprise in the dark eyes, she was hopeful. 'And how do you propose to pay for a lawyer's services?'

'I don't,' she said casually. 'I shall speak for myself. I'm more than capable.' He won't do it, she thought. He won't go that far. If he really cares for Paul, he won't do it.

She was wrong.

'Okay.' Arturo looked at his watch. 'I'll set the ball rolling as soon as possible, but it's too early to call anyone yet.' He paused, adding, 'I'm sorry it has to come to this, Carol.'

For whose sake? she wanted to ask. But it didn't matter. 'So am I,' she shrugged. 'Of course, there is one alternative.'

'Yes?'

'We could reach a compromise.'

'Like what? I'm listening, Carol.'

'Well, you were talking about hiring a housekeeper. Full-time. You'd probably need someone to live in, wouldn't you?'

'I'd definitely need someone to live in. I don't have a nine-to-five job.'

'Quite.' She glanced away, unsure how to phrase this. 'Well, I'd be prepared to act as your housekeeper.'

He didn't even attempt to hide his surprise. 'You?' he frowned. 'Are you suggesting we live together?'

'Certainly not!' She shifted uneasily. 'Well ... yes, but not in the way.... You put quite the wrong inflection on the words, Arturo. I'm talking about living in your apartment, working as a housekeeper so I can look after Paul personally. You know damned well what I mean.'

'Sorry,' he said flatly, 'the idea's impossible.'

Carol's heart sank. The more she thought about her idea, the less preposterous it became. It could, in fact, work. Couldn't it? They must at least discuss the possibility!

Arturo had gone into the living room and Carol went after him. 'Please hear me out. I know you don't really want to go to court. I know also that you will, if necessary. And so will I.' She was still sticking to her guns. 'But you did invite me to come up with an alternative, and I have. So please listen.'

He said nothing. He didn't even look at her.

'Our main concern is Paul. Arturo, you can give him a lot of things I can't give him—material things, mostly. I can give him time, attention, love. Let's forget ourselves for the moment and think of Paul. Surely this would be better than his being looked after by a stranger when he gets home from school—which would happen even if he lived with me in England. This way, you can keep him in America, which in itself seems to be important to you. Together we could give him more than we could separately. We could give him the best of both worlds.' She paused and then she went on for a few more minutes about the advantages to Paul.

Still Arturo was silent.

Carol's nerves were at snapping point. The stress and strains of the past few days had worn her to a frazzle and Arturo's lack of response was making her feel foolish now. 'Look, if there's someone in your life who'd object to this ... I mean, if you can't consider it because ... For heaven's sake, will you *say something*!'

He looked mildy surprised. 'But I've already told you it's impossible. You don't need to go on about the advantages to Paul, I'm well aware of them.'

'Then would you care to give me your reasons?'

'Not really.'

Exasperated, Carol came to the obvious conclusion. 'So there is someone in your life—a woman. Someone who wouldn't understand, who wouldn't accept the situation?'

'No. There's no one.'

Carol flopped into a chair, at a loss for words. Getting him to talk was difficult at the best of times; today it was like trying to extract a tooth from someone. Perhaps she'd shocked him beyond speech.

'It's a very shortsighted idea, Carol. I could live with it, but you couldn't.' This, after several minutes of silence!

'I?' She looked at him blankly. 'But it's my suggestion! What do you mean? I wouldn't change my mind after six months and leave! I wouldn't do that to Paul. I'm talking about commitment, Arturo. I'm prepared to make a commitment for Paul's sake. Why aren't you? If you care as much as you make out, if there isn't anyone else you have to consider.'

'You're a career girl. How could you be content to play housekeeper? What would you do with your spare time, the hours when Paul's in school?'

'That's a stupid question——'

'Answer me.'

Sensing that she was making headway, she answered him fully, hoping against hope that she could persuade him. 'I'd look after the apartment, I'd cook, I'd play tennis, I'd make friends, I'd read. And I can type. If I were bored, perhaps I could do some typing for you— your reports or whatever. I might even be useful in

Greenacres. After all, I have experience at coping with people who have problems. Oh, I don't know—maybe I can hold a basket-weaving class or something!' She laughed a little nervously, having no real idea of what she was talking about when it came to Greenacres. 'In exchange for all this, you provide the money—my keep, the housekeeping and so on. It seems perfectly feasible to me.'

'And what about your home? What if you're homesick? What if you miss your old lifestyle, the places you're familiar with, the people?'

Feeling more encouraged by the minute, Carol answered those questions, too, though she hadn't really given much thought in this particular direction. 'I'd have been more concerned about people missing me rather than me missing them. I mean the kids at the youth club, the people I deal with in my work. But I've already been out of their lives for almost six weeks, thanks to my illness. So the break has already been made. As for homesickness—have you ever been to Bolton?'

'No. I spent a few months in the south of England many years back, but I've never been to the North. I was on a short post-graduate course in psychiatry.'

She cocked an eyebrow at him. 'Taking some advantage of the British educational system, eh?' Before he could answer, she went on, 'Anyhow, swapping Lancashire for California won't be a hardship for me, Arturo.' Bolton for San Diego? She'd never seen San Diego, and California was a huge place, but what she had seen so far, she'd loved—enough to consider emigrating before now.

'And what about you and me?'

Now it was Carol's turn to think before she spoke. What of Arturo and her? 'Well, I—I don't suppose we'd see much of one another, would we?'

'That's no answer. I'd be living there too, you know.'

'Of course, but . . .' Was that amusement in his eyes? His dark, unshaven face was impassive, but—oh, it was so difficult to gauge what was going on in this man's mind. Why should he be amused, unless he was playing some sort of game with her? She tried to throw the question back at him, to see what he would say first, but it didn't work. He just raised his eyebrows and smiled slightly, waiting for her answer. But that was all she'd needed really, a moment in which to think. 'Bearing in mind that we wouldn't be living in each other's pockets, I think we could get along just fine,' she said truthfully. 'At the moment we resent each other, but when you think about it, it's nothing personal really. It's—well, almost a matter of principle. I mean, I've nothing against you . . . nothing at all . . .'

There was no doubt about it now. The ebony eyes were laughing at her. He got to his feet, very obviously putting an end to the conversation.

'Arturo! Where are you going?'

'To take a shower.'

She threw up her hands in frustration. 'Well, you might give me your answer, at least!'

'I will,' he grinned, 'when I come down.'

She stared after him and then made herself go into the kitchen and busy herself with breakfast. It was fair enough, he wanted to think about it. She had, after all, taken all night to think about it, but it must have come as something of a bombshell to him!

He came down wearing a white tee-shirt and plain black slacks. As far as Carol was concerned he might just as well have been naked from the waist up. The freshly laundered tee-shirt clung like a second skin to every muscle and contour of his chest and shoulders and, not for the first time, she acknowledged to herself that physically, at least, this man was very, very attractive.

She caught a faint whiff of tangy soap, a very masculine smell about him as she put a plate of bacon and eggs in front of him. 'Typical English breakfast.'

He was sitting at the kitchen table looking appreciatively at the food, but he didn't pick up his knife and fork until she, too, was seated. 'So you can cook, too. You seem very well qualified for the job.'

'I was hardly thinking of you in terms of being an employer,' she pointed out firmly. 'I was thinking in terms of a very civilised arrangement, a civilised solution to our problem. So, may I have your answer, please?'

'I have nothing against the idea in principle,' he said, meeting her really anxious eyes. 'But as I said at the start, the idea of our living together is impossible.'

Carol felt suddenly sick. The food in her mouth seemed to lose its flavour. His remarks didn't really make much sense, although the answer was clear enough. So what was she going to do now?

Arturo's eyes were still on her face. 'I've no objection to people living together, Carol, in this context or any other. But for a man in my position, it's out of the question . . . So will you marry me?'

Carol almost choked. *Marry* him? Had she misheard? No, no, she knew she hadn't. She put her knife and fork down and pushed her chair away from the table, feeling suddenly claustrophobic and hot. 'No. That was hardly what I had in mind.'

'It was the furthest thing from my mind, an hour ago,' he shrugged. 'But it's marriage or nothing.'

'But *why*?'

'I've just told you.' There it was again, that controlled patience in his tone which was his way of showing irritation. 'A man in my position, living in the annexe at Greenacres—think of the gossip!'

'Gossip? Arturo, you keep talking in terms of—I mean, I'm talking about a strictly platonic relationship! An arrangement!'

'I know that and you know that——' He didn't bother finishing the sentence.

'You mean all your patients would presume you were living with your mistress and a—what?'

'Illegitimate child, perhaps? Who knows what conclusions those with more colourful imaginations would jump to? Take that look off your face, Carol, you're not naïve. You must know how people gossip.'

'It's ridiculous!' she concluded. 'Ridiculous.' She poured herself another cup of tea for the sake of finding something to do with her hands. Carol was not easily embarrassed, not by any means, but for some obscure reason she could feel herself blushing now. 'Wait a minute. How did you propose to get over the problem of gossip if you'd hired a housekeeper? I mean, if we'd gone to court and you'd——'

'Quite easily.' He shoved his plate aside and looked at her directly. 'My idea of a housekeeper is someone fiftyish, someone motherly and plump, who bustles about in an apron. But if I'm living with an attractive twenty-four-year-old it'll make all the difference in the world.'

Carol looked down at her hands. She didn't think of herself as attractive. She was just average-looking. But the word pleased her, which was stupid, because he had no doubt used it for lack of another adjective. Still, she was a good deal younger than he. 'I see your point,' she conceded.

'Good. Now the ball's in your court. You said you were willing to make a commitment for Paul's sake. Did you really mean it?'

Heavens yes—yes, she'd meant it. But marriage was so . . . so serious. Marriage with all its implications. . . . What implications? How stupid to think like that! It would be a piece of paper and a ring, and a means of preventing gossip. Apart from that it would be meaningless. Except that it would guarantee that she and Paul stayed together.

'I meant it,' she said, in a voice which sounded oddly strained. 'The answer is yes.'

CHAPTER FOUR

A FEW days later Carol was sitting in the window seat of the plane which was taking her—and her new family—home. The plane moved along the runway at a terrific speed and then its nose tilted upwards and it soared away, cutting a path through the air, its enormous weight defying the laws of gravity.

Paul's fingers tightened around her own and Carol gave him a reassuring smile. She had expected him to want the window seat, but no, he had asked to sit between her and Arturo. The boy's face was still slightly bruised, although the cuts were healing quickly, as cuts do on young, healthy skin. 'Look, Paul,' she coaxed, 'see the planes on the ground and the buildings getting smaller and smaller?'

He glanced past her to the window and nodded, uninterested. A moment later he said, 'They—They're not really,' and then he closed his eyes, as if to let her know he didn't want to talk any more.

Carol held on to his hand and let him be. He had always been a talkative, lively little boy, and he would be again—she would see to that. It would just take time, that was all. When he did speak, there was sometimes a slight stammer in his voice now, or a tendency to repeat a word unnecessarily. And he was wetting the bed. He'd done so in the hospital and during the few nights he had been home—or rather, in the house which used to be his home.

Arturo had told her not to worry about either of these things, and she wasn't, particularly. Paul was insecure and afraid, and it was very understandable. She looked down at the coppery blondness of his hair, at the scattering of freckles on his nose. Paul was blue-eyed, as Sam had been, and very much a mixture of his parents. Ellen had been fair-haired and of medium height, very different from Carol, who took after her father.

She looked up to find that Arturo, too, was watching Paul. They were both aware that the boy wasn't asleep, but they made no attempt to force him into conversation. He had shown no excitement at the prospect of riding in an aeroplane, but he was glad, he'd said, that the three of them were going to live together.

Arturo's eyes met hers briefly, then he picked up the paperback he had bought at the airport, and Carol turned her attention back to the window. For the hundredth time, the thumb of her left hand ran over the cool, smooth metal which was the wedding ring on her finger. It felt heavy, alien to her, and she wondered how long it would be before its delicate weight felt natural to her, before the ring felt as if it belonged on her finger. It probably never would, given the circumstances which had brought this marriage about.

As the plane climbed higher and higher she looked down at the vast, sprawling mass of buildings which was San Francisco. They were flying south and on her right there was the sparkling, fathomless blue of the Pacific Ocean. A short time later, San Francisco was behind them. San Francisco and all the memories, good and bad, which that city held for her.

The past few days had flown by, but every detail, every minute of them was stamped indelibly on Carol's memory. They had been busy days. Busy, and following a logical sequence of events. First, she had written a very lengthy letter to her aunt and uncle, explaining what she was doing, that she wouldn't be returning to England to live. But she had only posted the letter the previous day, on the morning of the wedding. She had wanted to give herself a few days' respite before the inevitable phone call came from her aunt. Aunty Jean, more so than Uncle George, would think she had taken leave of her senses. She had explained everything, right down to the fact that marriage was necessary for Arturo's sake, in order to prevent gossip.

She had asked her uncle whether, assuming she gave him power of attorney, he would sell her flat for her complete with carpets and furniture. Arturo had stopped her worrying over this, explaining that it would be easy to arrange with her solicitor for her uncle to act on her behalf. She had asked Uncle George to sell her car, too. There was nothing complicated about Carol's affairs, the new car had been paid for by cash—which was the main reason she had been without savings to fall back on. In the letter, she had enclosed the key to her flat and a list of items she wanted her aunt to forward by air freight—some clothes and her cassettes and books. She had insisted that her aunt and uncle accept as a gift her video tape recorder in exchange for the favours she was asking of them. Of course they wouldn't mind doing what she had asked of them; they were the only family she had in England and they were very close to her. No, they wouldn't mind at all ... once they had got over the shock of Carol's emigration, not to mention her marriage.

Secondly, she had written to her boss enclosing a separate, formal letter of resignation which had been written in apologetic tones because she had been unable to give notice. She wondered what Marion, her boss, would think of it all, and the thought made her smile wryly. She had explained it all to Marion, who was a super person, but there was no doubt in Carol's mind that she, too, would think Carol had taken leave of her senses, marrying a virtual stranger.

Carol had cleaned her mother's house from top to bottom, leaving it spotless for the next tenant. She had brought with her a suitcase of mementoes, photographs, items of jewellery which she would never wear but which her mother had cherished. The unpleasant side of things, the disposal of clothes, furniture and the cars, Arturo had taken care of. He had spent a lot of time on the phone to San Diego, speaking to someone called

Max, who was one of his colleagues. He had dealt with the real estate company from whom Sam had rented the house. And he had made all the arrangements for their marriage. He had dealt with the licence, the documentation, the appointment for the necessary blood tests.

It had been a strange ceremony, if one could call it that, economical in time and words, with only Barbie Howard and her husband to witness the event. And Paul, of course. Paul, who had stood solemnly and silently, looking from one person to the next. It had been Paul's first experience of a wedding, and what a very bad example it had been, a coldblooded business affair as far as bride and groom were concerned, and that fact had no doubt been communicated to the man who had conducted the ceremony by the perfunctory kiss the bride and groom exchanged when it was all over. A kiss for appearances' sake. What the hell, when the wedding itself was purely for appearances' sake?

'Carol, would you like a drink?'

Arturo's dark brown voice jolted her back to the present, and Carol turned from the window to meet the eyes of the man she had married less than twenty-four hours ago.

'A drink,' he repeated. 'What would you like?'

'No, nothing, thanks. I'll wait till they bring coffee round.' She smiled at the hovering stewardess who was moving down the aisle, serving drinks from a trolley.

They didn't disturb Paul, who had let go of Carol's hand and was by now genuinely asleep with his legs curled up on his seat and his head resting against Arturo's upper arm.

'Are you all right?' Arturo asked. 'You don't get air sick, do you?'

'No, no, I'm fine. I was—I'm just interested to watch the scenery. We're flying over L.A. at the moment.'

'Lucky for you there are no clouds, then.'

Even a foreigner couldn't mistake Los Angeles, Carol thought. The size of the place! It made London seem small by comparison and it reduced Bolton to the size of a—a postage stamp!

Arturo fished in the pocket of the seat in front of him. 'Here, you can follow the route on this map, if you're interested.' He handed her the map and went back to his book.

Carol watched him from the corner of her eye, her stomach contracting nervously as she did so. He had been very co-operative, very efficient and helpful during the past few days. But he was, she had to face it, still a stranger to her. And she was going to live with him. . . .

Her mind jumped about like a grasshopper. She shouldn't have sent that letter to her boss, or the one to her uncle and aunt. It was too soon, far too soon to think of selling her flat, her furniture. She was burning her boats, wasn't she? And what if this turned out to be a ghastly mistake?

Before these thoughts had a chance to take a firm hold of her, Carol immediately put a stop to them. She refused, absolutely refused to think negatively. An optimist she was born and an optimist she would remain. It *had* to work! This—this situation, this arrangement, this ludicrous marriage, it had to work!

Think positively, she told herself again. Arturo is a perfectly reasonable man, even if he is something of a puzzle, and you'll get on just fine. Don't anticipate problems when there probably won't be any. Keep an open mind. So much will depend on your own attitude of mind, you know that. Worry will only beget more worry. Think how nice it will be to spend a lot of time with Paul—to have the freedom to do that. Think how nice it'll be to live in a place where the sun shines every day of the year. Well, almost! It does rain in California, despite rumours to the contrary!

She looked down at the map, her eyes flitting down the coastline depicted on it, picking out the names which sounded familiar as well as those which were famous ... Malibu, Santa Monica, Long Beach, San Clemente, and there, on the border of Mexico, was San

Diego. She couldn't find La Jolla, where her new home was, and she spent several minutes scanning the outskirts of San Diego wondering in which direction it lay. If La Jolla wasn't marked, it probably wasn't very big. She knew nothing about it except that it was a very prestigious place to live. Her mother had told her that.

'I'll show you where La Jolla is,' Arturo said suddenly, and she looked up to find he was watching her. How long had he been watching her?

Carol felt uneasy, increasingly so as Arturo leaned towards her, pointing to the map. 'It's about here. It isn't shown, but it's less than thirty minutes' drive into San Diego. There are plenty of shops in La Jolla,' he added. 'Not to mention beaches. You'll find everything you need there, I'm sure.'

Carol nodded and leaned back in her seat, grateful when he did the same. Quite apart from his size, the sheer physical power of the man, there was something about him which was almost ... dangerous. This realisation had come to her during the past few days, and while it was surely an exaggeration, she couldn't think of a better word. It was a stupid notion, perhaps, yet there was no denying that she felt disturbed when Arturo Kane was standing, or sitting, too close to her.

The journey went smoothly and Paul perked up considerably when they were going in to land at San Diego airport. Carol was glad of that, but for herself she knew only an increasing nervousness. How would she adapt to this new lifestyle? What would Arturo's colleagues think of her—of all of this? He had left San Diego a bachelor two weeks ago and now he had returned with a wife and a child!

Still, there could be no gossip among his patients, and that was the important thing. Arturo's authority, his standing in the community and his reputation as a respectable doctor were now safeguarded by that most honourable institution—marriage. Carol knew nothing of his hospital patients, but the ones under his care at Greenacres were a constantly changing community, to quote Arturo's words. Carol knew little about Greenacres, except that it was a private concern, an expensive place to stay, and that it housed twenty-five people plus the staff who lived in. There really hadn't been time to ask Arturo more about the place, about his routine. Tonight, perhaps, she would have the opportunity to do just that.

San Diego airport wasn't particularly busy, and they got a porter to help them with their excessive luggage—excessive because they had brought with them as many of Paul's belongings, clothes, toys, as was practicable. Including Mickey, who was not a mouse but a big, tatty teddy bear who sported a very incongruous bow tie.

They were half way across the car park, the porter walking ahead of them pushing a trolley-load of cases, when Paul announced that he wanted to go to the toilet. Carol looked at Arturo. This was his department. Besides, she hadn't the faintest clue where the lavatories were.

'Can't you wait till we get home, Paul? It isn't far.' The question came from Arturo.

'No.' They all stopped walking. Including the porter.

'Why didn't you go on the plane?'

'I did.'

Carol felt an overwhelming urge to laugh. It wasn't just because of the simplicity of Paul's retort, it was mainly the sight of Arturo. He was dressed in an immaculate, lightweight suit which fitted to perfection. In his right hand he carried an expensive, black leather briefcase and in his left arm, being carried as though it were a baby, the bear with the ridiculous bow tie! But it was the *way* he was carrying the thing which amused her most. 'Hadn't you better leave that with me?' She pointed to Mickey, suppressing her laughter because she was certain he wouldn't see the funny side of this. He was oblivious to the way he looked.

'What? Oh, yes. Porter . . .' he took out his wallet and handed a bill to the porter, 'see my wife safely into my car, would you? Here are the keys. It's that silver-grey Mercedes over there.'

He stuck his briefcase on to the pile of luggage, scooped Paul up into his arms and headed back to the airport building. The porter let Carol into the passenger seat of the car, loaded the boot and handed the keys to her. 'I should lock your door, ma'am, while you're waiting for your husband.'

As he tipped his cap and walked away, Carol gave vent to her laughter. Then she sighed, long and hard. Never mind me, she thought, how's he going to adjust to his new life? A thirty-six-year-old bachelor, used to living alone, whose life has revolved solely around his work. 'My wife', he had said. 'See my wife safely into my car.' It seemed he had adjusted to that fact, at least. The words had tripped so easily from his lips—or seemed to. Perhaps he had made a conscious effort. She would certainly have to make a conscious effort in referring to him as her husband, because she just couldn't think of him in that light, and never would.

Dusk had fallen, and though it was a long way off bedtime, Carol felt suddenly drowsy. It was probably a nervous reaction, or perhaps it was simply the warmth and comfort of Arturo's luxurious car. Whatever, she had trouble keeping her eyes open during the drive to Greenacres. She saw enough, though, to realise that San Diego was very different from San Francisco. On many of the buildings and houses there was a decidedly Mexican stamp, which wasn't surprising, considering that the Mexican border was just a few miles away. 'Were you born in Mexico, Arturo?' she asked, hardly realising she had voiced her thought. 'I mean, I know your mother was Mexican.'

'No.' He didn't take his eyes from the road. With something approaching reluctance, or so it seemed to Carol, he added, 'I was born in L.A.'

'I was born in a hospital,' Paul put in. And again Carol's laughter was a release of nervous tension. The impression she had formed of Arturo at her very first meeting with him hadn't changed: he was a very private person.

Greenacres was built on a plateau at the top of a gently sloping hill. It was a mansion, a huge white house built on three storeys. There was a broad stone pillar on either side of the main entrance and a wide verandah running from beginning to end of the front of the building. In the deepening dusk, beneath the light from a pale moon, it looked proud and resplendent. But Carol wasn't a girl who looked at things romantically; she was wondering if it would be a suitable place in which to bring up a child.

They drove slowly along a sweeping driveway, circled the house and stopped in a parking area at the rear. 'I won't bother putting the car away,' said Arturo. 'That's my—our apartment, over the garages. The entrance is quite separate from the main house, up those steps.'

She nodded. 'It looks nice, doesn't it, Paul?'

'I've been here before,' he said quietly, 'with—with Mom and Dad.'

'Yes,' Carol said softly, 'I forgot.'

The annexe had been built in keeping with the main building, from which lights were blazing behind closed curtains.

Arturo let them in to the apartment and flicked on the lights. 'There's a spare key in reception downstairs. You can pick it up tomorrow, then perhaps you'll have another one cut when you go into town.' He led them into the living room, turning on lights as he went. 'I'll get the luggage, leave you to look around.'

'I'll help you, there's so much——'

'No, you carry on.'

The hall they had passed through was small and square. The living room was large, very large, covered in beige carpet which was shag pile, wool, and ankle-deep. It went through the entire apartment and must have cost a fortune. On the plain walls were two Picasso prints and an original by someone whose name Carol didn't recognise. In the centre of the room, set at right angles, were two four-seater settees in dark gold corduroy material. In front of these was a smoked-glass coffee table. On one wall was a purpose-built unit which housed a hi-fi set, two speakers and a sizeable collection of records and cassettes. There were two matching lamp standards, several smaller lamps and a couple of armchairs flanking another glass-topped coffee table near the window.

Carol looked around with interest. The room was smart, simple and probably comfortable. But it lacked something. A splash of positive colour, perhaps? There was no warmth in it. Then she realised there wasn't a single plant in the room, not one ornament of any kind, nor was there a television. The room didn't look ... lived in. Everything looked brand new, unused. It was too ... orderly, absolutely spotless.

She heard Arturo putting luggage in the hall, his descent as he went to fetch the rest of it.

'I know where the kitchen is.' Paul tugged at her arm and Carol stooped to plant a kiss on his nose.

'Does that mean you're waiting for a drink?'

'Uncle Art won't have what I want,' he said, with a certain amount of distaste. 'The last time I came, he didn't have any pop! Not even one can.'

'Well then, you'll just have to settle for milk, won't you?'

The kitchen was superb, there was everything one could possibly want, from a dishwasher to an automatic washing machine and tumble drier to a waste disposal unit in the double-drainer sink. There was a fridge-freezer, a toaster, a mixer, a dozen cupboards, and the floor was covered in expensive, non-slip cork tiling in a matt finish. It was just about the most labour-saving kitchen one could dream of. But again everything seemed to be unused, though she knew Arturo could cook. The cooker itself looked as if it had been designed to cater for a small army: it was quite inappropriate for a bachelor.

The total contents of the fridge were two eggs and a

jar of beetroot. Of course there wasn't a drop of milk in sight. 'Damn,' Carol muttered under her breath, 'I didn't think about getting in some groceries.' Fortunately, in America one could go shopping at virtually any time of the day or night—but the prospect probably wouldn't please Arturo. They should have stopped on the way from the airport. One couldn't walk to the shops from Greenacres.

There were voices in the hall, Arturo's and that of another man. 'Carol? There's someone I'd like you to meet.'

She smoothed down the pleats of the simple navy skirt she was wearing, selfconscious because she looked very crumpled after the journey. Paul trotted after her into the living room.

'Carol, I'd like you to meet Max Brenner, friend and colleague. Max, this is my wife, Carol.'

Max Brenner stood as high as Arturo's shoulder. Just. He was slightly overweight and his colouring was not unlike Arturo's. His hair lacked that intense blue-blackness, although like Arturo, he had plenty of it. He wore a beard and his eyes were dark, but not dramatically so. They were friendly eyes, warm and readable.

He shook hands very firmly with Carol and when she told him she was pleased to meet him, she meant it. 'You've had a bad time, Carol,' he said quietly, so the words didn't reach Paul's ears. 'I'm sorry.'

For once, Carol didn't feel awkward at meeting a man who was considerably shorter than she. She always carried herself well and stood tall, proudly so, yet so often she felt ungainly when she towered over other people, especially men.

'Thank you.' Unlike Arturo, Max Brenner was easy to weigh up. In that instant of meeting him she knew several things about him: he was happy, content with his lot—whatever that was. It was not Carol's habit to make snap judgments on meeting someone new, but she felt instinctively that Max Brenner could be trusted. In the ensuing conversation, in which he made a point of including Paul, he said not a word about the marriage, and Carol was grateful for that. Congratulations would have sounded ridiculous, to say the least.

'Did the bed arrive?' Arturo asked as they all sat down. Turning to Carol, he explained, 'I asked Max to buy a bed for Paul.'

Carol nodded, saying nothing. She had seen three doors in the apartment, not counting the kitchen, and one of those had to be a bathroom. How many bedrooms were there? What, exactly, would the sleeping arrangements be?

Max frowned. 'Sure. It's in the den, okay? It should have arrived yesterday but it didn't, so I got on to the store this morning and spoke to them in short, sharp sentences.'

'Thanks.' Arturo grinned and Carol smiled inwardly. She couldn't imagine Max speaking to anyone in short, sharp sentences.

'You're a psychiatrist, too, I take it?'

'Yes, ma'am!' He broke into laughter. 'Ah, Carol, if you don't mind my saying so, I just love your accent!'

She smiled. He wasn't the first American to say that to her. 'Not in the least.'

'Hey, I have to go.' He looked at his watch and got to his feet. 'I'm on duty.'

'Problems?' Arturo looked up at him. 'You should have left here an hour ago.'

'No problems. Mrs Gregory's had a bad day, according to Kay, and she wants a word with me. Mrs Gregory's a new arrival.'

Paul got up then, sauntered over to Max and tugged at his jacket. 'I've seen you before, you know. Don't you remember me?'

'I sure do!' Max enthused, ruffling the boy's hair. 'I didn't think you'd remember me. You were only three years old when I last saw you, but I know you've been here since. So how old are you now. Four? Five?'

'Five and a half.'

'Wow! Oh, Carol——' Max tapped himself on the head, 'if this were loose, I'd forget it. Nancy, my wife, sent a few things over for you. Food. She told me to put it in your refrigerator and I clean forgot. Do me a favour, don't tell her that. It's in the trunk of my car. I'll get it.'

'Why, that was very sweet of her. Please thank her for me.' Carol got up. 'I'll come down with you, save you another journey.'

Max's car was in one of the garages beneath the apartment. Carol thanked him profusely for the two bags he handed to her, touched by the thoughtfulness.

'You're welcome. Nancy plans on calling to see you in the morning, is that okay with you? She thought you might like to find out where the shops are.'

'Yes, that's fine! I'm very grateful. Thank you . . . for everything.'

The warm brown eyes crinkled at the corners. 'Sure.'

Carol got on with dinner straight away. Nancy Brenner had sent the essentials: butter, milk, bread and the makings of a meal. And two cans of fizzy orange.

Arturo bathed Paul while Carol made up the new bed. It had been put into a small room which Arturo obviously used as a study. There were shelves lined with textbooks and a desk covered with papers, reports, files—all neatly stacked. But then they would be. If the apartment were anything to go by, Arturo had a tidy mind. She just wished she knew more of what went on in that mind.

It had come as a relief to her to discover there were two other bedrooms, each containing a double bed, the usual furniture and a wall lined with fitted wardrobes. She had not fancied sleeping on the settee. The bathroom in fact led off from the hall, and it was from that direction, to Carol's dismay, that the sound of Paul's crying suddenly broke into her thoughts. She went immediately to see what was wrong.

Paul stood before Arturo, who was kneeling, drying

him off with a towel. 'I—I d-don't want to go to a new school. I don't want to!'

'Let me tell you something,' Arturo said in a coaxing, confidential tone, 'you're going to the finest school there is in San Diego, and I know you'll like it. I promise you.'

'But all my friends are at the other school!' Paul stood listlessly, his bruised face pink with crying, and Carol stood in the doorway, her heart twisting inside her.

'You'll make new friends. You'll be in the same class as Max's little boy. So you see, you've got a new friend already.'

'But I don't know him! And I don't want——'

'Paul,' Arturo's hands came to rest on the boy's shoulders. His voice was quiet, gentle but subtly changed. It was no longer coaxing. It was firm. 'Everything will be all right. You'll start at the new school on Monday—no, look at me. You'll like it there, I know you will. Monday.'

The tears stopped. Paul looked very dubiously at Arturo, but the tears just switched off. 'Monday? How many sleeps is that?'

'How many what?'

Carol spoke up then. 'Sleeps.' She saw Arturo's look of surprise. He hadn't realised she was standing there. 'It's Paul's way of measuring time. So let's see, today is Wednesday ... Five more sleeps, Paul.' She stepped into the room. 'Actually, I think Monday is too——'

Arturo's look stopped her dead.

She held out a hand to Paul. '... I think Monday is a very good day to start. After all, it's the first day of a new week. Come on, bedtime.' She led Paul from the room, glancing over her shoulder to see Arturo straightening and chucking the towel into the linen basket. Their eyes clashed.

Paul went to sleep very quickly. The rubber sheet was in place in the bed and all he asked was that the lamp be left on.

Arturo was sprawled out on the settee when she emerged from Paul's room. It was a four-seater, and the length of him took up every inch of it. He looked over the newspaper he was reading. 'The next time you want to contest something I tell Paul, you'll do it in private, okay?'

'Okay.' She flopped tiredly on to the other settee. She'd known she was wrong and wasn't about to deny it. 'But I think Monday is too soon for him to start school. He's weepy, he's listless and he's still sleeping more than he should. I think we should give him a couple of weeks to get reorientated. Heavens, I'm feeling bewildered myself, so I can imagine how he feels!'

Arturo waited till she'd finished, attentive but obviously unmoved. 'Quite. So the sooner he falls into a routine, the better. I want him to get used to a new school before they break off for the summer vacation. Then he won't have a dread of going back in the fall. Apart from all that, he'd be bored stiff if we gave him two weeks off when there's no one to play with, when all the other kids are in school.'

It made sense. Carol admitted it to herself. 'And is he fit? Physically, I mean?'

'Medically, he's fine. And don't worry about the sleeping. That's just his way of reacting to the shock, the accident and ... everything else. What he needs right now is distraction. He'll get that in school.'

Reassured, Carol said nothing for the moment. It was rather handy, Arturo being a doctor. And he was a physician as well as a psychiatrist, of course. In fact, she hadn't realised how well qualified he was until she'd seen the string of letters after his name on the notepaper in his study.

'And, Carol,' he added, considering her, 'there are times when children need to be told what they're going to do, not asked what they'd like. There's security in being told what to do. Do you see?'

'Oh, yes,' she said reasonably. 'I've dealt with plenty

of adults who needed that, too. To be told what to do. To have things sorted out for them.' She paused. 'Well, I—I suppose I'd better go along and see the headmistress, or whoever. Where is this school?'

'Paul's already been given a place. I fixed it by phone before we left 'Frisco. They're expecting him on Monday. Which reminds me——'

'You arranged it by phone?' She was irked. 'You might have told me! You might have discussed it with me.'

Arturo picked up his newspaper. 'We had a lot of sorting out to do. There wasn't time to discuss every detail.'

She was irritated more by the gesture with the newspaper, by the way he was putting a full stop on the subject. 'Do you mind? There are several things I need to discuss with you now!'

'I'm aware of that.' He folded the paper and stuck it in the magazine rack at the end of the settee. 'I wasn't about to start reading. You can stop fighting me now, Carol. We're allies now, remember?'

'I'm tired.' She looked away from those all-seeing eyes.

'And scared?'

'Don't be ridiculous. Look, I—I'll get some coffee, then we'll talk. I want you to tell me something about your routine.'

Arturo's time, his week, was packed solid. He spent two days a week at the mental hospital, he had three half-day sessions at a general hospital in San Diego, where he saw outpatients, and he held group therapy sessions on two evenings a week elsewhere. He had private offices in the town, where presumably he saw his well-to-do patients, and which he shared with two other doctors, one of whom was Max. This was quite apart from the time he spent in Greenacres and the necessary paperwork he had to do. And another evening a week was spent lecturing.

Carol wrote it all down; she wanted to know when

she could expect him for meals and where she could reach him if it were necessary. Sam hadn't exaggerated about Arturo and his work; that much was obvious. So he was free on four evenings out of seven, by the look of things.

Unable to resist, Carol said, 'And you thought you'd have time to bring up a child? You must be joking!'

'I'm free all day Sundays,' he answered smoothly. 'At least, I can make myself available. And I have every intention of delegating some of that work now that Paul's here, although that's probably easier said than done. It might take a while. Now—you'll need a car. Tomorrow's out of the question. I'll be leaving early and I'll be home at six, but keep Friday morning free and we'll go into town and buy you a car. I'll call my bank tomorrow and have an account opened for you into which I'll put an allowance every month. That'll cover housekeeping, clothes for Paul and your own needs. I'll arrange to get credit cards for you, too. In the meantime . . .' he got to his feet and took all the cash from his wallet, 'that'll see you through the next couple of days. You'll need to buy food and things.'

Carol glanced at the bills he had laid on the coffee table. 'That's too much, Arturo. I don't need all that.' She was a little embarrassed by all this, although it was, of course, the agreement they had made.

'Take it. Now, is there anything else?'

If there was, she couldn't think of it at that moment.

'Do you mind if I have the bathroom first? I've got an early start in the morning.'

'No, I—that's fine.' Carol watched him as he went into his bedroom. The three bedroom doors opened on to the living room and his was next to Paul's. Actually, Paul's bedroom had probably been intended for use as a study or perhaps a dining room. But the dining table and chairs were in the kitchen, so they would obviously take their meals in there.

When Arturo came out of his room, Carol felt a ripple of shock run through her. She avoided looking at him, picked up the pen and started doodling on the pad which was still on her knee.

'I meant to ask you what you think of the apartment.' He walked over to her, standing just a few paces away, perfectly at ease, perfectly relaxed.

Carol forced herself to look up at him, to meet his eyes. It was just too ridiculous, she told herself, feeling like this. Arturo was bare-chested. In his hand there was a towelling bathrobe, but he was wearing only the trousers to the suit he had had on. Although she had shared a house with him for almost two weeks, she had never actually seen him undressed before. Whether he had avoided that deliberately or whether it was simply that he felt freer in his own home, which was how it should be, she didn't know. Whatever, it was a disturbing sight. Very. Arturo Kane was a magnificent physical specimen. His bronzed skin was polished and smooth, his chest covered by a mass of black, silky hair, and Carol found herself wondering what it would be like to touch and whether his body would feel as solid as it looked. Curiously enough his chest looked even broader naked than it did when he was dressed, even in a jacket. And there wasn't an inch of excess weight on him. No doubt he burned up energy at a terrific pace, the way he worked. The chest tapered off to a taut abdomen and firm hips.

His trousers were not tight; they were perfectly cut, but from the way he was standing, Carol could see the shape of powerful thigh muscles and it required little imagination to visualise what he would look like completely naked. She saw it all, even though her eyes were kept determinedly on his face.

'Yes,' she said casually. 'It's a nice place. I like it.'

'Well, I hope you'll feel free to alter things, if you want to.' He was, of course, oblivious to her scrutiny.

'I will,' she said bluntly. 'I intend to make one or two additions, here and there.'

'Fine.'

She wished he'd go and get on with his shower, or

whatever, but he stood for a moment, looking around the room. She would have to get used to it, the reality of living with a man. The reality of living with anyone. For six years she had lived alone and prior to that there had been her mother. Her mum, her friend. Things would be very, very different here. . . .

'I'm not sure how well it's going to work out,' Arturo was saying, 'living here. For a start, it's very inconvenient having only one bathroom. We'll have to see how it goes.'

Carol didn't answer. She didn't want to prolong the conversation. An hour later she climbed into bed in a state of exhaustion, yet sleep did not come readily. Had she been utterly crazy to marry Arturo? Should she have insisted on just living with him? No, she couldn't have. He would never have bought that, for his own reasons. People would have talked, there was no denying it. As Arturo had pointed out, she was eleven years his junior.

The irony was, though, that since they were man and wife, people would naturally assume. . . . . Ah yes, now she was getting to the nitty-gritty. She laughed at herself, aloud, the sound of it hollow in the darkness of her room. People would naturally assume they were lovers. *That* was the irony. But it wouldn't be like that, married or not.

Carol turned over and thumped her pillow into a more comfortable position. So much had happened, there had been so much to do since the decision about the marriage had been made, that she hadn't had time to think about the reality of living with Arturo. She did find him attractive; if she had suppressed the idea before, there was no denying it now. Oh, but that was the last thing she wanted. Complications such as that she could well do without. She had quite enough to adjust to as it was.

Something else occurred to her, too. She still couldn't honestly say whether she liked Arturo. Ludicrous though it was in the circumstances, the most she could say was that she didn't dislike him.

Anyway, what was she worrying about? He felt exactly the same way about her, she was sure of that. Neutral. No more, no less. There was one major difference, though. Arturo did not find her physically attractive. She was glad of that; it was quite a relief.

So perhaps in time they would become friends. That would probably be the ideal. She would try to work in that direction because at the moment there was still awkwardness between them. Well, for her there was. It would be so much nicer for Paul if the atmosphere in the home were friendly. At the moment, she and Arturo were strangers who were polite to one another. She really must make an effort to do better than that.

In the moments before sleep claimed her, Carol felt all her old confidence returning. The talk she had just given to herself, and the one she had given herself on the plane, had straightened out her mind. She would simply take each day as it came and avoid looking for problems where there were none.

CHAPTER FIVE

CAROL woke with an awareness that someone was standing in her room. Her eyes came open quickly and it was seconds before she realised where she was, not to mention who she was.

'Are you awake?'

'I am now.' She pulled herself into a sitting position. Paul was standing by the bed, holding Mickey by the ear. 'What time is it, darling? It must be very early.'

'I don't think so. You've got a clock on your table. The little hand's on seven and the big hand's on two.'

'It's early.' Carol laughed. She could easily have slept till noon. 'Where's Uncle Art?'

'I don't know. Shall I see if he's in bed?'

'No, no, you stay right there, young man.'

'I've slept in that bed,' He nodded towards the bed as Carol registered that his pyjamas were missing. 'With Mom and Dad. When we came to visit. Carol, Carol . . .' his voice trembled and she knew what was coming, 'I've—you know—I've done it again.'

She waved a dismissive arm. 'That's all right.' Arturo had told her, quite unnecessarily actually, to make light of this little problem. 'Everyone does at some time or other.'

'Not grown-ups.'

Her laughter was genuine. 'It has been known.'

'You won't tell them, will you?'

'Tell who?'

'The people at school.'

'I won't tell anyone,' she assured him. 'But it really doesn't matter, you know.' Quickly, seeing his alarm, she added, 'I promise I won't tell anyone. Not ever.'

They finished their unpacking together, Paul's clothes fitting with ease in Carol's spacious wardrobes. That was something she had forgotten to mention to Arturo; she would have to buy some furniture for Paul's room.

By eight-thirty they had breakfasted, made the beds and the washing was spinning around in the machine. It was a luxury for Carol, having a machine; she had hated her once-weekly trips to the launderette. Arturo hadn't been in bed, of course. He must have left the apartment at some ungodly hour.

When the phone rang, Carol picked it up and read out the number on the disc.

'I'm sorry,' a female voice said, 'what number did you say?'

Carol repeated it.

'Yes, but who is this?'

'Mrs Kane,' she said politely, thinking it might be a patient. 'Mrs Arturo Kane.'

There was a sudden silence and Carol looked at the receiver. 'Hello? Hello?'

'Doctor Kane's wife?' The voice had changed. It was a distinctive voice, too. American but not Californian, though Carol couldn't place the accent, except to say that it was Southern. Patiently, politely, she asked if she could help.

'No! I'm sorry . . . I've got the wrong number.' And with that, the woman hung up.

Carol shrugged and put the receiver down.

'Who was that?' Paul asked.

'A wrong number.' She turned around quickly as she heard someone coming into the apartment. Arturo wasn't expected home till six. . . .

'Oh, good morning.' A middle-aged woman had let herself into the apartment with a key, looking as nonplussed as Carol.

'Good morning. Er—who are you?' It was hardly likely to be Nancy Brenner, she felt sure of that.

'Mrs Polowski,' the woman said. 'They didn't tell me there'd be someone in here.' She stopped as she caught sight of Paul. 'Oh, you poor little boy, what's happened to your face? Did you fall?'

Paul stepped smartly behind Carol's legs. 'Mrs Polowski, would you mind telling me why you're here? And why you have a key to Dr Kane's apartment?'

The woman's mouth opened and closed. 'I'm the cleaner. I work six till nine downstairs and then I always come up here for an hour to do the doctor's rooms. I—I get the key from reception.'

'I see.' Carol smiled. She was irritated over the remark about Paul's face, but it wasn't the cleaner's fault. The woman had obviously been told nothing, nothing at all. Furthermore, Carol didn't want a cleaner coming in for an hour every morning; the apartment would be simplicity itself to keep clean. But she wouldn't say or do anything yet.

'Well, let me introduce myself. I'm Carol Kane, the doctor's new wife. And this is Paul. My—my husband didn't mention you'd be calling, but please carry on, Mrs Polowski. Please do whatever you normally do.'

'Yes, Mrs Kane.' The woman slipped her jacket off and Carol found herself wondering whether she ought to keep her on. She looked as if she might really need the money. Her accent was heavily Polish, her hair greyer than it should be and one could see from her hands that she had done too much cleaning in her time.

'If you'll let me have the key,' Carol said nicely, 'I'll get another one cut while I'm in town today, and then I'll put yours back in reception, okay? Thank you. And please help yourself to some coffee, there's plenty in the percolator.'

'Thank you, ma'am. You're not an American lady, are you? Everyone calls me Mrs P., by the way. It's easier.'

'I'm English.'

'Oh, that's nice! I'll—I'll get on now.'

Carol felt rather stranded. She wondered what time Nancy Brenner would arrive, but she busied herself by sorting out Paul's toys while Mrs P. vacuumed. It was only then that she realised what was bothering her about the phone call she'd taken. It hadn't been a wrong number! The penny had only just dropped; the caller had said, 'Doctor Kane's wife?' And Carol had made no mention of a doctor.

So who was it? She ran over it again in her mind. Obviously it was someone else whom the grapevine hadn't reached. But the woman had been taken aback, to put it mildly, which made it very unlikely that it was a patient.

Of course it wasn't a patient! Arturo's patients wouldn't ring this number when there was an office downstairs and his secretary in an office in San Diego.

It wasn't difficult to put two and two together. It was someone from Arturo's personal life. An American woman with a soft and very distinctive voice. A woman who had been shocked into silence on learning that Arturo had married.

Hadn't Arturo assured Carol that there was no woman in his life who would object to this marriage? Or was Carol putting two and two together and making five?

Nancy Brenner arrived at ten-thirty. On the dot. Mrs P. let her in and Carol greeted her in the living room. 'Mrs Brenner—Nancy?' It's very kind of you to come. . . .'

The woman extended her hand. 'And you're Carol. It's lovely to meet you. I can't tell you how pleased I am about——' She stopped as if she'd been about to say something tactless. 'But I'm so sorry about your parents, Carol. They were nice people. I met them a couple of times.'

'Thank you.'

'And this is Paul.' Nancy's face broke into a smile as Paul emerged from his room. 'I bet you don't remember me, mm?'

'I do!' Paul said proudly. 'You're the lady with nice hair. Like—like my mom's.'

'Such a gentleman!' Nancy laughed, skipping over the

subject of Paul's mother. 'I can see you and I are going to be great pals!'

The little boy looked pleased by that, and Carol smiled warmly at the other woman. Her hair was not unlike Ellen's in style, it was short and soft and naturally curly. But Nancy was decidedly blonde, far more so than Ellen had been. She was slim and petite with laughing eyes, very green eyes. Her pale green dress was gorgeous, sleeveless, straight and simple. It was the sort of thing women's magazines described as 'casual day wear', but it hadn't been bought in a chain-store. That much was obvious even to Carol, who wasn't interested in clothes. There was something decidedly expensive-looking about Nancy Brenner; she was one of those women who had natural flair and good taste.

Carol motioned her to sit down. 'I understand you have a little boy, Nancy?'

'I've got three.'

'Really? All boys?'

'Yes.' She looked heavenward. 'They're a handful at times, but I adore them, really.' She smiled at Paul. 'Darren's my youngest. You and he will get on just fine, Paul, I'm sure of it.'

'How old is he?'

'The same as you, exactly. He's five.'

'But I'm five and a half.'

'Oh!' Her laughter was warm, throaty, almost gurgly. 'Sorry!' She winked at Carol. 'I forgot the half. Which is very important, of course.'

'Of course! Would you like some coffee, Nancy? There's some already perked.'

'Well, actually I thought we'd stop for coffee when we're shopping. Unless you're not ready to go yet?' A little suspiciously she added, 'Did Max tell you what time I was coming?'

'Er—no. But I'm ready when you are. I'm looking forward to seeing La Jolla.'

At which point Paul proceeded to tell Nancy how

Max forgot to put the food in the refrigerator the previous night.

Carol gave him an admonitory look. 'Paul——'

'Don't worry about it.' Nancy shook her head, her vivacious face reflecting her amusement. 'You can't keep secrets with children around. Trust Max! That can't have done the butter any good! It must have turned to oil!'

They chatted easily, comfortably, for another ten minutes or so before they got round to leaving. Small talk, of course, but Carol was glad of it.

As they were leaving the apartment, Nancy asked whether Carol had had a chance to look around Greenacres yet.

'No. It was getting dark when we arrived, but I've every intention of exploring the grounds. They look sumptuous. How many acres are there?'

'Five. It's a sumptuous place altogether. A good word, that. We'll go in, now, and I'll introduce you to the nurses.'

Carol was dubious, wondering whether Arturo would want to make the introductions himself. As if sensing this, Nancy smiled reassuringly. 'The staff have been forewarned, don't worry. Art told Max to let them know he was bringing a wife back from 'Frisco.'

'And a child?'

'And a child.' They were walking around the house towards the main entrance when Nancy suddenly put her hand on Carol's arm. 'Carol,' she said quietly, her face serious now, 'just remember who you are. Remember that you don't owe anybody an explanation. I—hope you don't mind my saying this?'

'Not at all,' Carol said gratefully. 'I appreciate it.' She did, too, in more ways than one. It showed her that there was no need for any kind of pretence with Nancy Brenner; it brought out into the open what Nancy knew full well, that this was purely a marriage of convenience.

The young woman behind the reception desk greeted

them pleasantly and courteously. 'Mrs Brenner. Mrs Kane—How do you do?'

Carol explained that she was taking the spare key in order to have another one cut, and before she had finished speaking, another woman appeared and greeted Nancy very formally.

The other woman was Kay Sharpe, and Carol could feel her resentment even before Nancy had finished making the introduction. Kay Sharpe was the nurse in charge. She was a little older than Carol and almost as tall, an attractive woman with auburn hair.

'Mrs Kane,' she nodded, not proffering her hand. 'Welcome to Greenacres. This has been quite a surprise,' she smiled, 'for all of us.'

Mainly you, Carol thought, noticing the falseness of the smile. Nurse Sharpe was the first person to make any such comment, and Carol was wondering how she should answer it when Nancy stepped in.

'A lovely surprise, isn't it? Mrs Kane would like to take a look round, Miss Sharpe.'

'By all means. I'll leave that to you, shall I?'

'No.' Nancy's delicate brows rose as she smiled politely. 'I'd like you to give us a guided tour.'

Nancy had said it on purpose. Carol knew that, but she wasn't sure why—until she saw Kay Sharpe's face tighten in annoyance. 'Of course, Mrs Brenner.'

It didn't take long. Carol was introduced to several other members of staff as they moved from room to room. Greenacres was an idyllic place with a nice, restful atmosphere. The décor, the furnishings and its facilities were all geared towards relaxation, towards its function as a halfway house. Carol was shown one of the bedrooms, too, which happened to be empty.

'There's a new guest arriving this afternoon,' Kay Sharpe volunteered.

Carol noted the use of the word 'guest', and the way the staff were dressed in ordinary clothes instead of nurses' uniforms; the only way of separating them from the 'guests' was by looking to see whether they were wearing a name-badge. The badges, too, said Mr, Miss or Mrs instead of 'Nurse', though they were, in fact, all medically trained.

Kay Sharpe answered Carol's questions, and there were plenty of them, politely enough but the other woman's resentment was unmistakable. Carol found herself growing irritated by the unfairness, not to say stupidity of this, not knowing what she had done to offend.

When they came back to the reception area, she thanked the woman as a matter of course. 'Well, thank you for showing me round, Nurse Sharpe. It was very interesting.'

'Miss Sharpe,' came the crisp reply. 'As I explained, we don't want to make our guests feel like patients any more. By the time they come to Greenacres they've had enough of that; in most cases, anyway. They're well on the road to recovery and they don't want to be reminded that they're still being nursed.'

'Yes—quite.' So consider yourself told off, Carol thought.

'Of course you're not American, Mrs Kane?'

'No.' It was an unnecessary remark, coming from her, because she had obviously been put in the picture and the information must have included Carol's relationship to Paul and her nationality. 'I'm British.'

'Ah, yes, of course.' There was that false smile again. 'Your accent . . . I should have realised. You have such a strong accent.'

Time to assert yourself, Carol thought, bearing in mind Nancy's advice. 'Why, Miss Sharpe, what a strange thing to say!' She smiled and let amusement drift into her voice. 'I'm English. *You're* the one who speaks with an accent. Goodbye.'

Nancy held on to her laughter until they were all seated in her car and were half way down the drive of Greenacres. Then it just bubbled out of her. 'Beautiful, Carol! You handled her beautifully. Good for you. Oh, I enjoyed that!'

'Is she always like that?'

'No. Though I've never taken to her myself.'

'Why was she so resentful of me, then?'

Nancy took her eyes from the road. 'Can't you guess?'

Having been challenged to think about it, it became obvious. 'She has designs on Arturo.'

'You'd better put that into past tense, now he's married.' Nancy gurgled delightedly.

Carol didn't know about that. An obvious marriage of convenience was hardly likely to stop the woman. Casually, she asked, 'I wonder how Arturo responds to that?'

'Ha! He probably hasn't noticed, knowing him. I'd guess that half his female patients have designs on him, too. Of course, that's pretty common, you know, with psychiatrist and patients. Attachments are formed. Even Max has his fans. I shouldn't worry about it.'

'I'm not,' Carol said quickly, truthfully.

'Art doesn't even like Kay Sharpe at a personal level. But she's really good with the patients—excuse me, guests. Really good. I'll say that much for her.'

'Has he told you,' Carol asked, in spite of herself. 'That he doesn't like her, I mean?'

'Lord, no! Art wouldn't volunteer that sort of information.'

That figured. Arturo volunteered as little as possible about anything, especially his feelings.

'I didn't like that lady.' Paul, sitting on the back seat, quiet till now, put in his two-penn'orth.

Nancy and Carol exchanged looks, realising they'd better drop the subject of Kay Sharpe in view of children's propensity for repeating what they hear.

Shopping in American supermarkets was an adventure in itself, a little tiring, quite bewildering but fascinating. The foodstores had everything one could possibly want, with masses of it and dozens of brands to choose from. Everything under one roof.

Carol allowed herself to be guided by Nancy as she

bought food for freezer storage, fridge and general groceries. Nancy had a huge coldbox in the boot ... the trunk ... of her car, so there was no particular hurry for Carol to get home in order to put things away.

Next, they drove to the centre of town and did a little exploring on foot, Nancy pointing out this shop and that shop, hotels and buildings of interest. 'We'll go back to the car now and I'll show you the beaches—oh, Carol, look! Wouldn't that suit you? It's perfect for you!'

They were strolling down Girard Avenue and Nancy had stopped to peer in the window of a very expensive-looking boutique. The window was sparsely but tastefully dressed and there were no price tags on anything. 'Do you think so?' Carol looked dubiously at the red silk dress draped over velvet on the floor of the window. 'I never buy red. I don't think it's my colour.'

'But red's exactly right for you, with your colouring, that dark brown hair! And it'd add some colour to your complexion, too.'

Carol grimaced. 'Yes, I am whiter than white, aren't I?' She was, compared to Nancy who had a golden tan and an enviable glow about her. She was a pretty woman, too, and she obviously knew about make-up—though Carol never bothered with make-up.

'Never mind, summer's coming. You'll soon pick up a tan,' Nancy said kindly. 'Let's go in here and you can try that dress on!'

She was so enthusiastic that Carol felt almost guilty for saying no. 'Really, I will have to think about buying some clothes to suit the climate, but that's strictly evening wear. Besides, I dread to think how much it costs.'

'But this is a medium-priced shop,' Nancy shrugged. 'It wouldn't be outrageous. Anyhow, your new husband can well afford it!'

And what, Carol wondered, would her idea of outrageous be? Very different from Carol's, she felt sure. Still, she had warmed to Nancy Brenner, who had been kindness itself. Not as instantaneously as she had warmed to Max, but she certainly liked her. 'No,' she said quietly but firmly. 'Maybe you're right about the colour, I don't know, but it's not my style. I'm too tall, too thin for that sort of dress.'

'I wish I were taller,' Nancy said wistfully. 'I feel even shorter walking next to you. I'm a regular five feet two.'

'And I feel gawky and awkward next to you,' Carol said bluntly, which amused the older woman no end.

'Lunch,' said Nancy, when she had recovered. 'We've left it awfully late. You must be hungry.'

'I am,' a little voice piped up.

'Oh, darling!' Carol stooped to pick Paul up. He was not only hungry but obviously tired. She felt guilty for having dragged him round the shops; he must have been so bored! But he'd made no complaint at all. 'Let's skip the beaches today, Nancy. We'll find somewhere to have lunch and then Paul's likely to fall asleep.'

'My place. We'll have lunch at my place, then I'll drive you home.'

'Oh, I don't want to put you to more trouble——'

'It's no trouble at all. I have a cook.' Nancy grinned as they approached her car. 'And we'll be home in a few minutes. Hop in.'

'Don't you live in the hills? I'd just assumed you lived near Greenacres.'

'No. Near the beach. Just a minute, Paul. Let me push that box out of your way. All right, honey?'

Nancy's house was a surprise, to say the least. It was timber-framed, vast and rambling. At the side of the house there were hard tennis courts and the surrounding gardens were a blaze of colour.

At the back of the house there was a swimming pool, and it was near that, on white garden furniture, that they sat down to take lunch. Nancy had shown Carol round the house while lunch was being prepared—Paul having settled in the garden with the two big dogs who had come bounding up on their arrival.

'Oh, Nancy, this is lovely!' Carol looked round, still amazed by it all. The house and grounds were slightly elevated, overlooking the ocean. Wasn't it sheer extravagance to have a pool when the beach was just a couple of hundred yards away? 'How nice to sit outside to eat. It's so beautifully sunny today!'

'Well—yes, I suppose so.'

'And your home is lovely!' Privately Carol wondered how Nancy reconciled expensive antiques and glassware with the presence of three young sons. Wasn't that a bit risky? But the house was a home and not a showplace. It was a combination of comfort and quality. She wondered how much Max earned that he could provide a home like this. A uniformed maid had greeted them, a cook had prepared lunch, and Nancy had mentioned that her boys' nanny would be picking them up from school. 'Fancy having your own swimming pool, too. You are lucky!'

Nancy looked at her curiously then, her voice rather selfconscious. 'Yes, I—I suppose I am.' Quietly, and as if it it had only just occurred to her, she added, 'I—I rather take it all for granted, I'm afraid ... Oh, Carol, I wish I dared to eat a second potato! Go on, go on, have some creamed cheese on it. You can afford to! More wine?'

'No, thank you. Now there's nothing wrong with your figure. You're not one of these women who's always dieting, are you?'

'Yes. My figure's only reasonable because I work at it like mad. So does Max, though he's less strict with himself!' She smiled fondly, amused by her thoughts.

'Can I go and play with the dogs again?' Paul drained his glass of orange juice and got up from the table.

'Of course,' said Nancy. 'They'll be glad of some exercise. Don't worry, Carol, they're big dogs, but they're as soft as anything. Absolutely ruined! He'll be quite safe with them. ... Now what was I saying? Oh yes, at my age, weight creeps on very insidiously. I'll be forty this year, isn't that a depressing thought? I'm a year older than Max, you know.'

'No, I didn't realise that.' Carol helped herself to yet another baked potato and another portion of tuna salad. 'How long have you been married to Max?'

'Twelve years. And I'm just as crazy about him now as I was then. It took me a long time to get him, I'll tell you. He refused to marry me at first.'

'Really? How come?'

'My money. Ridiculous, isn't it? I'm wealthy in my own right, you see. Max accused me of being a Boston 'aristocrat'—that's where I come from originally— who'd been spoiled by old, inherited money. Silly devil! But he'd only recently finished all his training then and he wasn't earning much. He was just starting to get established, you know. He refused to live on my money and he refused to marry me when I asked him to.'

'You asked him?' Carol was fascinated. 'So what happened?'

'I got pregnant.'

'You mean, deliberately?'

Nancy looked a little sheepish then. 'Yes. Naughty, wasn't it? It was a gamble. Max was hopping mad about it. He knew I'd done it deliberately, of course.'

'And?'

'And so he married me. Pretty soon he was earning good money and now, well, he's really landed. He no longer objects when I spend my own money. The gamble paid off. We're really happy.'

Carol had had the feeling Max was a happy man the moment she'd met him. It showed in his eyes, somehow. Unlike Arturo, who.... She thought of her own gamble then. Of the gamble they had both taken for Paul's sake. 'Did you know Arturo in those days, Nancy?'

'I met him shortly after I came to California and started going out with Max. But he and Art go back a long way. They served their internship at the same hospital, although Max was a couple of years ahead of Art, of course, being that much older. Yes, they go back as far as high school, actually.'

This came as something of a surprise to Carol. She found herself wishing she knew half as much about Arturo as Max must know. 'So you're really good friends.'

'Oh, yes. In fact, we're the only people Art socialises with, really. He spends so much of his time working! What with the hospitals and his voluntary work. . . .'

Carol was wondering about Arturo's social life. There was someone he saw, other than Max and Nancy Brenner, even if Nancy did seem oblivious to it. She was thinking about the woman who had phoned that morning. So what, anyhow? She didn't think for one minute that a man like Arturo lived like a monk.

'Voluntary work? What voluntary work?'

'Didn't he tell you?' Nancy frowned. 'He works in San Diego two evenings a week.'

'Yes, but——'

'He does it for nothing. And you should see the area he works in! I tell you, I wouldn't like Max to be in that part of town at night. It's very rough, to say the least. Mind you, Arturo's hardly a potential victim for muggers—the size of him! He's a beautiful man, isn't he?'

Carol said nothing. She was thinking how ludicrous it was to be married to a man she knew so little about. She pushed her chair away from the table a little and turned her face towards the sun.

How different the lifestyle was here. In these circles, at least, it was luxurious and easy. Then she thought of the people in Greenacres, the people Arturo was seeing right now at the hospital, and those he helped voluntarily. Poor people, probably, who couldn't afford a doctor of his status. And she thought of the cases she had dealt with at home and of her own life in Lancashire.

It was nice, not to *have* to go to work. It was super to sit in the sun by the splendour of the Pacific Ocean. It was nice to shop and to socialise with someone warm and friendly like Nancy Brenner. But what would life be like from now on? She couldn't do this every day, and even if she could, she didn't want to. She, too, wanted to do something useful. She'd been trained for that and it was in her nature, besides.

'I was asking, Carol, do you play golf?'

Startled, Carol shook her head, managing somehow to suppress laughter. Golf? Even if she could have afforded such a hobby, it had never appealed to her. 'No. Why?'

'I just wondered if you'd like me to introduce you around the golf and country club. Max and I are members, though he hardly gets a chance to go there, and when he does it's usually for a quick game of squash with Art. But I go two or three days a week to play golf. I love it.'

'Nancy, thanks ... but no.' Carol had no wish to offend, but she felt she must make it clear to Nancy that she just wasn't that type. 'You see, I want to find my feet, if you know what I mean. I'm really hoping I might occupy myself in Greenacres for a couple of hours a day. If I can be at all useful, that is. And if Arturo will agree. I don't want to commit myself to anything else, nothing at all, until I—until I know. . . .'

Nancy prevented her from struggling any further. 'Understood,' she said softly. 'I keep forgetting how you've really been thrown in at the deep end.'

'I don't mean to sound——'

'You don't sound anything other than honest. You're straightforward, I've learned that much about you! And I like that. Of course you want to find your feet. Here you are in a new life, in a new country, with a ready-made family. I admire your courage, Carol, It's taken a lot of guts to do what you've done.' She glanced over at Paul, who was out of earshot, playing on the other side of the pool.

'Well——' Carol shrugged, 'thank you.' She hadn't thought in terms of courage, but, 'It applies to Arturo, too. He's plunged himself into a new lifestyle.'

'Yes,' Nancy agreed. 'And we've always known how

fond he is of Paul, but even so. . . . Well, Max and I never thought he'd marry again.'

'Again?' It was a few seconds before the words registered. 'Marry again? I didn't know——' Carol's voice trailed off at the look on Nancy's face; she had paled noticeably.

'You—you didn't know?' she floundered. 'But—but what about the registration of your marriage? Your marriage licence? It must state somewhere that Arturo was a widower? You must have seen——'

Carol felt sorry for her, at the way she was regretting her slip and, now, making matters worse. 'No. Arturo dealt with everything. I didn't see any papers. He's got the licence. I didn't see or hear anything when I married him, I just made the necessary noises. You can imagine how nervous I was, how scared. . . . Of course it doesn't matter, Nancy. Heavens, don't look so worried!'

Did it matter? Not to Carol, no. It was a surprise, but that was all. She had taken it for granted Arturo was a bachelor—Sam had never mentioned that Arturo had been married. But then why should he? It was obviously some years ago.

'Please,' Nancy implored, 'don't say a word to Art. I shouldn't have mentioned it. I'd just assumed you knew.'

It was Nancy's concern, and nothing else, which gave the matter added importance, and Carol was bemused at her reaction. 'I shan't say a word, I promise. Stop worrying.' To keep things light, and in an effort to change the subject for Nancy's sake, she picked up the threads of their earlier conversation. 'By the way, while I'm not the golfing type, I do enjoy an occasional game of tennis.'

Nancy didn't seem to hear that. 'Arturo would be really mad if he knew you'd found out from me. I—I can't understand why he didn't tell you himself.'

There was something about Nancy's voice which told Carol she had a very good idea why Arturo hadn't mentioned this himself. She was curious now, where she hadn't been curious before, but she didn't pursue the matter; Nancy's discomfiture was all too plain and she didn't want to put her on the spot. Her second attempt at changing the subject worked. 'Nancy, I'd be very grateful if you'd come shopping with me when I buy some new clothes. I've been unwell recently, so I want to wait until I've gained a few pounds and got back to normal—but how about it?'

'Done!'

It worked like a dream. The subject changed to clothes and Nancy went into the house to fetch a bikini she had bought a couple of days earlier, saying she wanted Carol to see it. She came back wearing it, lamenting because none of her swimwear would fit Carol and the younger girl had to remain clothed in her rather drab skirt and blouse. As they chatted, they moved over to the sun-loungers near the pool and Nancy discarded the top half of her bikini. Carol blinked at that, but it was obvious from the even tan of Nancy's body that she made a habit of sunbathing topless. And why not? She was in the privacy of her own garden and they weren't overlooked. When her boys came home from school and the maid came out with jugs of orange juice, nobody batted an eyelid, including Paul.

Introductions were made all round before the children went up to the games room in the house, and it was Nancy who remarked how nice it would be for Darren to have someone of his own age to play with. Her other boys were aged ten and eleven, and tended to consider Darren a baby.

Carol and Paul left at around five and as soon as Nancy dropped them off at the apartment, Carol immediately put all her shopping away and prepared the food for dinner. Fortunately, she didn't actually start cooking her and Arturo's food, which was just as well, because she got a phone call from Arturo, saying he would be home around nine instead of six.

She fed Paul, bathed him and put him to bed. There

was no question of a bedtime story tonight, he was so tired after his very full day. Carol waited for her husband and enjoyed the silence of the apartment. She was never lonely when alone; on the contrary, she liked having a certain amount of time to herself, and she had always been able to have that, living alone.

When it got to ten o'clock, however, she became rather twitchy. Arturo was an hour later than he had said he would be. In fact he was four hours later than the time he had originally given her. Perhaps he was catching up on his paperwork. There must have been a lot to do after his two weeks in San Francisco.

He came home at ten-thirty. Carol was just coming out of the bathroom and she hadn't heard his key in the lock. She came face to face with him in the small hallway. 'Oh! I didn't hear you come in.'

When he said nothing, she looked up at him curiously. 'Is everything all right?'

'Fine. I'm sorry I'm so late. Sorry about dinner.' He dropped his briefcase on to the hall table and moved past her, into the bathroom.

He had been drinking. Probably not much, because he certainly wasn't the type who would drink and drive. But there had been a whiff of alcohol on his breath. Brandy, if she wasn't mistaken. So much for him doing his paperwork!

Walking into the kitchen, Carol thought quickly about what she should say to him, if anything. She wouldn't mention his previous marriage, of course, because she had promised Nancy and because it was not relevant to her. But there was something else, now, and Carol found herself mildly irritated by it. Arturo had been with a woman this evening. Now what would be her wisest course of action, to mention it or not?

'What are you doing?' Arturo joined her in the kitchen as she switched on the cooker.

'Starting dinner.' She edged away slightly. He was standing too close for comfort and when his hand closed over her bare arm, she stiffened.

He let go of her at once. 'I don't want anything to eat. It's too late. I didn't realise you'd wait dinner for me.'

'That's okay,' she said lightly, still affected by his nearness and cursing herself for the stupidity of it. 'I'll just make myself a sandwich. I—I'll join you in a minute.'

She took her sandwich to the living room, but her appetite had diminished, probably because she had waited too long. Or was it due to the confusion she was feeling at this moment?

'How did you get on with Nancy?' Arturo put his feet up and loosened his tie.

'Super. She and Max are nice people, aren't they?'

'The best. So tell me about your day.'

Carol paused, looked at him levelly, then made up her mind in split seconds. 'I had an odd phone call this morning,' she said without preamble. 'From a woman. Someone who was stunned into silence when I told her I was Mrs Kane. . . . And at a rough guess, I'd say it was the same lady you've been with tonight.'

The dark eyebrows rose sardonically. 'Indeed?'

'Arturo, you've got a lipstick smudge on your collar. And none of this is my business,' she added quickly. 'But you told me there was nobody—no woman— who'd care about this marriage, and there is.'

Quietly, thoughtfully, he said, 'I believed I was telling you the truth. I didn't realise. . . .'

The sentence was never finished and Carol waited for nothing, growing more uncomfortable by the minute. 'Your affair is your affair, Arturo. I'm not asking you to tell me anything about it, let's be quite clear on that. But—Oh, dear! I—I didn't know whether to mention this or not!' She looked to him for a word of encouragement, or even discouragement, but he said nothing. 'Look, I've no wish to alter your life more than is absolutely necessary. I mean, I've come into your life for reasons . . . I don't want to. . . . All I'm asking of you is discretion. You obviously have a lady

Love, romance, intrigue...all are captured
for you by Mills & Boon's top-selling authors.

TAKE FOUR
EXCITING BOOKS
ABSOLUTELY FREE

Four exciting Mills & Boon
Romances have been specially selected
for you to enjoy FREE and without
any obligation. You'll fall in love with
the fascinating characters, the
intrigue and the exotic locations of
these marvellous stories. Each
romance will hold you spellbound
from the first page to the last
loving embrace. To find out how
you can claim your FOUR FREE
BOOKS, please turn over.

See overleaf
for super offer.

Mills & Boon, the world's most popular publisher of romantic fiction invites you to take these four books free.

FOUR BOOKS FREE

friend and I realise. . . . What I'm saying is that if—if you're discreet, I see no reason why you shouldn't carry on——'

'You've arrived at a lot of conclusions since that phone call, haven't you? Carry on, you say? That's very—er—modern of you.'

'Well, I don't expect faithfulness from a man within a platonic marriage! I am a realist, for heaven's sake!'

He smiled. It was a mixture of scepticism and amusement. 'Forget that phone call. Forget the whole thing. Don't worry about it any more.'

'I wasn't,' Caro shrugged. 'And I hope you haven't finished—I mean, I hope you haven't done anything rash on my account!'

'I don't act rashly,' he pointed out. 'Any more than I would act on a whim.'

Unsure how to answer that, Carol took her untouched sandwich into the kitchen. She didn't linger. 'I'm going to bed, Arturo. I—didn't mean to pry.'

'You haven't,' he shrugged. 'I've told you, forget about tonight.' He waved a dismissive arm, obviously wanting to drop the subject. 'Goodnight, Carol,' he said nicely. 'Sleep well. Remember we're going to buy you a car tomorrow. We'll make an early start, right?'

Carol nodded, smiled at the stranger who was her husband, and escaped into the privacy of her room. Lord, how little she knew of him! And how much had come to light in one day; she had learned that he had been married years ago and was now having an affair with someone. Or had he finished it, in fact? He didn't actually say, he had just told her not to worry about it. Did that mean he would continue, with the necessary discretion now he was a married man? Or would the fact that he was married prohibit the continuation of the affair? Carol honestly didn't care one way or the other. With Arturo's aversion for gossip, the consideration for his professional position, she knew he would be extremely careful if he continued with this woman—

whoever she was. And that would automatically protect Carol from gossip, too. And the woman.

On balance, she hoped he would continue his affair. She was, as she had said, a realist. In its crudest terms, and though this might be a terrible injustice to the woman involved, a man needed a sexual outlet. Arturo wasn't interested in Carol in a physical sense, that she was certain of, but if ever he did make an approach to her, she would have no illusions over what it meant.

As she climbed into bed, she smiled at herself. Implicit in her agreement to marry was the fact that she would provide Arturo with meals, clean linen and a tidy apartment. And that was all.

You fool, she chided herself. You complete and utter fool! Do you think for one minute that you'd be able to resist if Arturo made a serious pass at you? When your pulse accelerates if he's merely standing too close to you?

Irrelevant, irrelevant, she told herself. It wouldn't happen. Hadn't she drummed into herself the fact that she mustn't look for problems where there were none?

The very last thing Carol expected was for her little half-brother to bring up the subject! But sure enough, when they were all in the middle of breakfast the next morning, he did.

Suddenly, quite out of the blue, Paul looked up from his plate and glanced from Arturo to Carol. 'Why don't you two sleep in the same bed? My mom and dad did.'

Carol's fork stopped in mid-air. For once, she was really stumped. She looked to Arturo for help only to see that the ebony eyes were sparkling with laughter. 'Eat up, Paul,' she said, 'we want to leave soon to go shopping.'

'But why?' This time, the question was directed specifically at her since she had been the one to answer. 'Married people always sleep in the same bed.'

'Not always,' she said smoothly, avoiding her husband's eyes and damning him for his silence. 'Some people prefer to have a bed each because—because there's more room.'

Paul thought about that for a moment. 'Oh.'

'Allow me.' Arturo beat her to the teapot, compelling her to meet his eyes while stopping her from finding something to do with her hands. He wasn't smiling but his eyes were. 'Well done,' he muttered, and she couldn't prevent herself from grinning.

So there was, it seemed, a sense of humour in him.

CHAPTER SIX

'CAROL! Sit down, sit down. How did it go with Mrs Gregory?' Max Brenner beamed at her from the other side of the desk in his office in Greenacres.

'Fine, just fine.' Carol lowered herself into a plush leather armchair and nodded in satisfaction. The Mrs Gregory Max referred to had been staying at Greenacres for a month. While there was nothing drastically wrong with her, she was a very, very depressed lady.

At Max's request, Carol had driven Mrs Gregory into La Jolla so she might shop for a birthday gift to send to her mother-in-law, and, on Max's instruction, she hadn't left Mrs Gregory's side for a moment.

Carol's own birthday, her twenty-fifth, had been and gone during the second week of May, but she hadn't mentioned it to anyone. She had been at Greenacres nearly four weeks, and life had settled into some semblance of order. Paul was loving his new school, much to her relief, and his bed-wetting and stammering had almost stopped.

As for the apartment, Arturo had moved his files and books into his office here in Greenacres and they had bought some furniture for Paul's room. They had bought a television for the living room, mainly for Paul, and Carol had made the few additions she had promised herself. They were just little things: she had bought another painting, a few plants and some colourful scatter cushions, and she had replaced the white lampshades with some of a softer hue. The room looked warmer, cosier—indeed, Arturo had remarked on it, approvingly.

It was Max who had first asked her to do something to help out at Greenacres. The secretary he and Arturo

shared with another doctor at the offices in San Diego
had been off sick for a couple of days and Max had
wanted to send off a few urgent letters. He had drafted
them by hand (almost illegibly) and had asked Carol to
type them for him, which she had done on the
typewriter in Greenacres' reception.

Whether those letters had really been urgent, or
whether it was just Max's way of making Carol feel
useful, she would never know. Whatever, she was
grateful to him, because things had taken off from there,
and she came downstairs almost daily now. She would
type the menus or do some filing or man the
switchboard. Sometimes she played cards with some of
the patients, or walked around the grounds with them
and made small talk. Or she would just listen while they
talked. Whatever they needed.

Almost everyone staying at Greenacres was well-to-
do, and Carol had learned that the problems of the rich
were just as real as were the problems of the poor. They
were merely different, or sprang from different causes.
Apart from one man, Mr Reeve, who never spoke and
spent all his day reading, Carol had chatted to
everyone. She still thought of these people as patients,
they were patients, even though they were not referred
to as such.

Kay Sharpe resented Carol's presence, she knew that,
but it was just too bad. She seemed to resent the way
Carol had fitted in so easily, and Carol had done that
not only with the patients but with her new life. She
was—and she had thought about this carefully—as
happy as she could hope to be.

She had burned her boats, too, as far as England was
concerned. Aunty Jean had telephoned from Bolton on
receipt of Carol's letter and had implored her not to sell
her flat just yet, to see how things went in California.
At first Carol had agreed, simply because it was
undeniable common sense. But in the middle of last
week, when Arturo said he thought they should start
looking round for a house, she had phoned her uncle

and asked him to set the ball rolling for the sale of her car and flat. After all, if Arturo was talking in terms of buying a house it meant that he was satisfied with the way things were going, didn't it?

'Did Mrs Gregory say anything you should tell me about?' Max asked. 'Did she say anything about herself?'

'One thing.' Carol nodded. 'She was obviously nervous and lacking in confidence, and she didn't talk much at all. But she did take care in choosing a gift, and when we were coming up the drive just now she said she was going to ask you if she might go home for the weekend. Perhaps next weekend.'

Max thought about it for a moment and then he grunted. 'Good. I'm very grateful to you, Carol. It's sweet of you to give up your own time for something like this, but we can't always spare the nurses, and Mrs Gregory wouldn't have coped without a chaperone. You know, a lot of lay people are intolerant of what's called depression, but the term can embrace so many things. . . . Anyhow, what about yourself?' He fiddled with his beard, his kindly eyes smiling at her. 'How's the driving going?'

'Amazing,' Carol chuckled. 'For the first couple of days, I thought I'd never get used to driving on the wrong side of the road.'

'The right side of the road, if you don't mind!'

'Mm! But I've adjusted surprisingly quickly—which is just as well!' She was driving a small Volkswagen, similar to the one she had had in England, and she was happy with it.

'By the way, I hear you and Nancy had quite a riot at the shops on Saturday?'

'Riot?' Carol mused. 'I'll bet that's Nancy's word. I thought so! Do you know we almost came to blows at one point? Your wife needs restraining, physically, when it comes to buying clothes, even for someone else!' Carol laughed at the memory. Oh, but she'd enjoyed herself. She had bought seventeen new garments and she still hadn't spent her monthly allowance from Arturo. At first she had refused to try on some of the things Nancy picked out for her. Their taste was so different. But Nancy had a keen eye for what suited a person and when Carol had tried on the dress she was wearing now, she had stopped arguing and allowed herself to be guided by Nancy. As a consequence, she had ended up with clothes more feminine, more colourful than she would have chosen herself—and she was thrilled with them.

She had postponed her shopping until she had regained her lost weight. Actually, she had even gained an extra four pounds, to her astonishment. And though she was nowhere near as brown as Nancy, she had acquired a light tan. She was looking . . . not bad, after her first month in La Jolla. Not bad at all.

Max was laughing, nodding, affirming. 'Who're you telling?' Then he sobered. 'And how are things going, Carol? With you, I mean.'

Her smile was wry. With her and Arturo, was what he really meant. 'You've seen for yourself, Max. We're polite to each other, even friendly at times.' She took a deep breath, finding she could summarise the situation precisely. 'Arturo's a gentleman, Max. He's controlled. He speaks only when there's something worth saying. Oh, he answers all my questions, but he volunteers nothing about himself. He's a generous man—very. With money, at least. He's easy to please as far as my cooking's concerned, he always tidies up after himself— even on the mornings when he gets up very early and makes his own breakfast. I really can't say he's difficult to live with.'

'But?'

There was silence.

'But nothing,' she said airily.

More silence.

'All right.' Carol sighed. 'We—we live separately together, if you can understand what I mean. Still, we'd more or less agreed on that. The important thing is that

Paul's doing well.' She paused, wondering how much she could say, should say. Then in a rush, she added, 'Arturo is the most undemonstrative person I've met. That isn't a criticism, I'm just stating a fact. He—what can I say? He remains emotionally untouched and untouchable.'

Max's hairline rose about half an inch, his eyebrows went up and he looked at her as if he'd never seen her before. 'No, Carol, no! You're absolutely wrong about that last point. Dear me. . . .' He shook his head, positively upset.

Carol felt a little guilty. She hadn't really meant the last thing she'd said about Arturo. Really, she had been testing Max for a reaction; she was seeking a confirmation or a denial or her own opinion. An opinion of Arturo which was based on so little evidence. 'I—Max, I'm just telling you my impression. Or rather, the impression Arturo gives. I mean, he never, never, talks about his feelings, not even in the smallest way. Dear God, I don't even know whether he likes me or not! I'm not sure whether he merely tolerates me or—oh, I don't know!'

'Carol, Carol . . . wait.' Obviously troubled, Max laid his hands flat on his desk and kept his eyes down. Seconds passed before he attempted to answer her. 'It's true, Arturo isn't demonstrative. It's—his professional detachment carried over into his personal life. No, no, it's more than that; it's in his control, it's the way he chooses to be. But don't make the mistake of thinking he's emotionally untouched or untouchable. Behind that cool veneer is the most sensitive man one could ever hope to meet. There is nothing—no human condition or emotion that he cannot understand and sympathise with. His feelings, his passions, run very deep.

'Arturo is . . . how can I put this? He's deep water. Beneath that placid surface there are hundreds of currents at work. But you'll never see a break on that surface. He spends his life listening to other people's troubles, and for himself he asks nothing.'

Disturbed, Carol held up a silencing hand. She had her confirmation. She was hearing the truth, she knew. Only now was she fully realising, fully recognising what she had known—more or less—for almost six weeks. And now she was thinking of the anger, the fury, she had once caught a glimpse of. . . . 'Yes. Yes, I understand. I—I think I've known this all along.' She raised troubled eyes and smiled thinly. 'I once saw a break on that surface. I know his passions run deep. It's just the impression he gives, of coolness, of. . . . I—I just wish he'd talk to me now and then, about what he feels, about what goes through his mind.'

Max smiled sadly. 'Carol, he doesn't even tell me what's going through his mind—though most of the time, I can guess.'

'Lucky you. You know him thoroughly well, don't you?'

'We've been friends since we were kids. I was ten when I met him, and he was eight.'

'Eight? I didn't realise you went back that far. That was when he moved in with his Uncle Sam, wasn't it?'

Max clicked his tongue at the inaccuracy. 'That was when his mother abandoned him and left him, literally, on Sam's doorstep in the middle of the night, yes.'

Carol's jaw dropped. She had known nothing of this. Sam had never told of the circumstances which had brought Arturo to live with him. 'How—how did he feel about Sam?'

'As a teenager, he idolised him. As a man, he loved him like a father. You wouldn't know he's mourning, would you? I bet he never batted an eyelid at the funeral.'

There was no need to answer that one. Max knew. It was only when she caught Max looking at her hands that Carol realised how tightly she had been twisting them together. She released them, seeing the imprint of fingernails in her palm. 'I'd better go.'

'Just a minute,' Max said softly. 'You were seeking

reassurance, and I haven't given you any. So let me say this: you're an exceptional girl, Carol, intelligent and sensitive. And don't think for one minute that your specialness escapes Arturo. He likes you, all right. Furthermore, he trusts you. He'd never have married you otherwise.'

'Thanks. But let's have no illusions about his reasons for marrying me! I mean, come on!' Laughing, Carol got to her feet. 'However, I'll take your word about how he feels now. Since Arturo's never likely to tell me, I'll have to, won't I?' She shrugged and glanced at her watch. 'Max, I really must go. I'm taking over reception for a couple of hours while Patti goes to the dentist.'

'Fine. Hey, don't forget you're all expected for brunch on Sunday. Bring your tennis gear and your new bikini.' He winked as she looked at him in surprise. 'Oh, yes, I heard all about that from Nancy!'

Tutting, Carol headed for the door. 'Is nothing sacred?' And then a thought struck her and she turned to look anxiously at Max.

'Yes.' The warm brown eyes swept over her face, reading her thoughts. 'Conversations such as this, for instance.'

Acting purely on impulse, Carol retraced her steps, walked around the desk and planted a swift kiss on Max's forehead. 'Thanks again.'

For a moment he looked like a little boy, so pleased by her spontaneous gesture. Then he frowned. 'You should try doing that to your husband.'

'You must be joking——'

'It wouldn't do any harm at all.'

'And it wouldn't do any good, either. Look, this conversation got out of hand, got a little heavy. I'm happy enough, Max. And Arturo seems to be. Paul certainly is. I don't want you thinking there's a problem. I was just—chatting. You asked how things were and I told you, all right?'

'Sure.' He said it lightly enough, but it was as if he were also asking why she was protesting so much.

'You psychiatrists!' With a gentle slap on the shoulder, she turned to go. 'You analyse too much! Everything's fine, *really*! I'll see you on Sunday. 'Bye.'

Patti Morgan, the receptionist, was waiting for her. 'Good morning, Mrs Kane. Oh, nice dress! Is it new?'

Carol glanced down at the red and white polka-dot dress she was wearing. 'Yes—thank you. I hope I haven't delayed you, Patti.'

Patti Morgan was a friendly girl with whom Carol got on very well. They spent a couple of minutes going over the reception books, in one of which was recorded patients' appointments with Max and Arturo; Arturo was due at Greenacres at two that afternoon.

'There's a new guest coming at lunchtime today,' Patti pointed out. 'Or thereabouts. One of Dr Kane's.'

Carol became aware of someone standing behind her. It was Kay Sharpe, saying nothing but just looking on.

'It's a Miss Goldman,' Patti went on. 'She'll be staying in room twelve. Now, I must dash, Mrs Kane.'

'Good luck at the dentist's.' Carol waved her off and turned to face Kay Sharpe. 'Did you want me, Miss Sharpe?'

Kay Sharpe smiled, not as hostilely as she had during Carol's first couple of weeks, but still resentfully. 'I just wanted to ask you if you'd let me know when Miss Goldman arrives. I'll be in the staff room, probably, having lunch.'

'Yes, of course. And my husband's arriving at two. He asked me to let you know he'll want a word with you.'

'Thank you, Mrs Kane.' She said it respectfully, impeccably, then walked briskly away and left Carol to it.

The telephone rang. It was yet another phone call from some poor female who rang regularly to enquire about the man who never spoke, who spent all day reading. 'I'm sorry,' Carol said gently but firmly, 'he isn't taking telephone calls yet, but he's doing well. . . . Yes, if you'd like to speak to Dr Brenner, I'll put you through. Just a moment.'

The first hour passed without incident but at a little after one, the peace and tranquillity of Greenacres was disturbed for the first time in Carol's experience when a long black limousine pulled up directly in front of the main entrance.

The beautifully polished doors of the mansion were open, as usual, and Carol glanced up and saw the car, blinked and looked again. It was the longest car she had ever seen, and she had seen some fancy ones here in America. It had three sets of doors and it gleamed in the midday sun, the brilliance of the sun deflected from the highly polished blackness of the paintwork. A uniformed chauffeur stepped out and held open the rear doors to allow the exit of the most beautiful, glamorous woman Carol had ever set eyes on.

The woman was wearing a full-length white mink coat, and though it should have looked ridiculous in a California June, on her it didn't. It looked—right. She was perhaps in her mid-thirties, blonde and beautifully made up. From Carol's vantage point, she couldn't yet see the tension, the whiteness of the woman's complexion beneath the make-up.

Then a second passenger got out. It was a girl of sixteen, maybe seventeen, and she looked like nothing on earth. Her hair was orange, cut severely short, in a crew cut, dyed to a crisp. She was wearing red running shoes, pink socks and a denim boiler suit under which there was a grey blouse.

The woman said something to her chauffeur, who got back into the limousine but didn't move it, put her arm around the girl's shoulder and promptly had it shrugged violently away.

The two females approached the reception desk and Carol put on her reception face. 'Good afternoon.'

The woman was older than Carol had thought; she was forty plus and her face was familiar, though Carol couldn't immediately place it. Despite the fine lines which were visible in close-up, she was undeniably beautiful. Oh, but the unhappiness, the worry that was reflected in her eyes. . . .

'Good afternoon. I'm Mrs Goldman and this is Sandy, my daughter.'

'Shut up, Mother,' the girl snapped. 'I'll do the talking.' Her eyes flitted around the reception area, then came to rest on Carol's face. 'Crummy,' she said.

Carol wasn't sure whether the pronouncement was aimed at herself or at Greenacres. 'Ah, Miss Goldman, we're expecting you. I'm——'

'I'm not interested. Not interested in you or in this——' There followed a stream of abuse in which the girl very inaccurately described Greenacres. It was punctuated three times by her mother saying, 'Sandy, please. *Please!*'

The girl laughed, coarsely, raucously, jerking a thumb towards the woman in mink. 'This is my mother, Madeline Gold. You recognise her, of course. And I am Madeline Gold's daughter. That's what you may call me—Madeline Gold's daughter, okay?'

The girl was frightened; Carol had seen that instantly. Beyond the tough voice and the bravado, her fear was plain to see in the trembling of her hands, the whiteness of her face, the eyes which flitted about, unable to hold still. And she looked ill, almost emaciated.

Carol looked straight at her, tried to hold her eyes. 'I think I'll stick to Sandy. It's much less of a mouthful. *Okay?*'

The girl shifted on her feet and the mother looked alarmed.

'Goddammit, where've you come from?' Sandy demanded. 'What kind of accent is that supposed to be?' She shrieked with laughter. 'English, isn't it? Did you ever hear anything like it!'

'Sandy——'

'Shut *up*, Mother. So, English, in case you're not familiar with American television, American movies, I'd better introduce you.' She made a dramatic, expansive gesture with her arm. 'This is my mama, Madeline Gold. She's the has-been of the casting couch, favourite lay of all leading men, a little lined, a little ageing, but still making pots of money on the big and small screens.'

Carol cringed inwardly. Oh, the girl didn't shock her, but she felt desperately uncomfortable for Mrs Goldman. That poor woman, who was now looking at Carol helplessly, almost with pleading.

'Sandy, we've reserved room twelve for you,' Carol said pleasantly, 'and our Miss Sharpe is waiting to meet you. I'll call her and she'll show you to your room.'

'—— your Miss Sharpe,' Sandy swore. 'Where's the *spic*?'

'I beg your pardon?'

'I beg your pardon,' she mocked. 'The spic. The big Mex. Where is he?' When Carol looked blank, she went on, 'My Mexican shrink, the big guy—where the hell is he?'

It was seconds before Carol realised Sandy was referring to Arturo. 'Dr Kane's expected at two. He'll see you this afternoon, Sandy.'

'Look, you, the price he's charging to keep me in this—this morgue, he might at least be here to meet me!' Her voice rose shrilly then. 'He's *my* shrink and *Madeline* here is paying for his services, so get him on the phone right now and tell him I need him!'

There was the sound of laughter from behind. Low, rumbling laughter which was familiar and unfamiliar at the same time. Carol turned to see Arturo standing in the doorway to the office which led off from reception, to her left. He must have come in by the back entrance and how long he had been standing there, unseen by all of them, she had no idea. She was just grateful he was there.

'Sandy. . . .' Arturo spoke the name slowly, shaking his head and smiling as if he were just delighted to see the girl. 'Your reception committee awaits.' He bowed his head slightly, leaning casually against the doorjamb, his arms folded across the broad expanse of his chest. 'How was your journey?'

The girl stared at him, and Carol saw her mother's shoulders drop with relief. Then Sandy grinned. 'You need a face transplant.'

'So you've told me.' Arturo flashed a smile at her quite unlike anything Carol had seen before. The ebony eyes moved fleetingly to Carol and on to Mrs Goldman. 'Mrs Goldman,' he moved round the reception desk and proffered his hand. 'It's good to see you. How are you?'

'Dr Kane.' The woman was nearly weeping with relief and Carol looked from one person to the next. 'I—I'm well, thank you. Our journey was—Sandy was sick and we had to stop for a while, but. . . .'

'But you made it.' Arturo finished for her. 'Let me introduce you to my wife.'

When the introductions were made, Sandy looked very sheepishly at Carol. 'I didn't realise who you were,' she muttered.

Arturo held out his hand to the girl. 'Sandy, welcome to Greenacres.'

Sandy looked—oh, so many things. Delighted. Uncertain. Afraid. Defiant. Admiring. Mainly the latter. She took Arturo's hand and shook it. 'Go to hell, Dr Kane.'

Arturo shrugged. 'Tried it once, didn't like it. Sandy, go and ask the chauffeur to bring in your luggage. Unless, of course, you don't want to stay in my— morgue?'

The girl flushed bright pink and without another word, she did as she had been told. On Arturo's instruction, Carol buzzed Kay Sharpe and within minutes Mrs and Miss Goldman had been led upstairs.

Arturo stayed with Carol for a moment. 'You handled that well,' he said. 'I heard all of it. It seems you're unshockable, Carol.'

'Pretty much. Miss Goldman has a whopping crush on you, you realise?'

'It happens. It'll wear off.' He glanced at his watch. 'Her mother's staying just long enough to see her settled in. I want to talk to them both, separately, and have words with Kay. So I'll see you later. Are you picking Paul up at the usual time?'

'No. He's staying at school for a swimming lesson. He'll be an hour later than usual.'

Arturo turned to go. 'Good. That'll give me an opportunity to talk to you, only I won't have a chance tonight. I have to go into San Diego.'

'Will—will you be eating at home?'

'No.'

Carol let him go. She didn't ask any more questions. This should have been one of his free evenings. Well, it *was* one of his free evenings. So how was he going to spend it—and with whom? She pushed the question to the back of her mind, reminding herself that it was really none of her business. In the month that she had been married to Arturo, she had learned enough about his routine to realise that it wasn't always strictly adhered to. Sometimes he worked at the hospitals or at his offices for longer than expected and sometimes, like today, he arrived somewhere early. In other words, Carol thought, he has or he can make for himself a few hours' spare time here and there.

Despite herself, when Patti came back from the dentist she was still thinking about this. She went up to the apartment and made herself a light lunch, then tried, unsuccessfully, to read. There was nothing to do in the apartment.

Was he continuing his affair with the woman with the soft, distinctive voice? Naturally, she was curious and she had wondered about it several times. But there was a difference now, suddenly. Suddenly, the thought of it bothered her far more than it should, given the strangeness of their marriage. She wouldn't ask Arturo about it. Never again. And she was damned if she'd permit herself to feel jealous, but the truth was she felt. . . . What, exactly?

Carol didn't analyse any further. Remembering with pleasure the new clothes she had bought, she took herself into the bedroom and had a session of trying them all on again, enjoying herself like mad.

The emerald green bikini, one of two that she had bought, was really too brief, she decided. She looked at herself in the full-length mirror of her wardrobe, weighing it up from all angles. The way the briefs were cut was very flattering, making her hips seem more shapely and her legs endlessly long. She pulled the slide from her hair, shook her head and held her hair up on her crown, posing and laughing at herself. Then she let her hair drop around her shoulders and pulled a face at herself. There was no way she would take this suit to Max's house on Sunday. It was too brief. In fact it had been a waste of money; she'd probably never have the courage to wear it. Shame.

Picking up a few strands of her hair, she inspected the ends closely. Split ends. She needed a trim. How long was it since she had had her hair trimmed? She must ask Nancy about a hairdresser—get half an inch taken off the bottom.

'Very, very nice.'

The deep voice caught her completely off guard and she spun round to find Arturo standing in the doorway. She felt shocked, idiotic, and she snapped at him, 'That's the second time today you've crept up on me! I thought you were working?'

'I'm through.' His eyes moved slowly over her body. 'I did knock just now, but I guess you were too busy to hear me.'

Carol looked away, feeling more idiotic. Had he seen her posing routine? Until now, she had managed to keep herself to herself. She had seen Arturo half naked plenty of times, but she had never let him see her anything other than fully covered. 'I'll never wear this,' she said, almost defensively. 'It's bordering on the . . . on bad taste.'

The expression amused him. 'I don't agree. But it

wasn't the bikini I was referring to. I was admiring you, actually. You have a beautiful anatomy, Carol.'

Anatomy? Laughter bubbled up in her throat but she suppressed it. Just as she managed, somehow, to prevent the blush which was threatening. She dug her nails into her palms and took a deep breath, unaware of the provocative rise of her breasts as they strained against the nothingness which was the bra of the bikini. She would *not* blush. 'You wanted to talk to me, of course.' She nodded, waving him away. 'Please excuse me, and I'll get dressed.'

He frowned at her tone of voice. 'You needn't be so uptight. I'm a doctor, remember? I've seen plenty of bodies in my time.'

'Perhaps. But that's hardly the point. Would you mind, Arturo?'

He grinned, vanished, leaving Carol with trembling hands and a too-rapid heartbeat. She moved quickly, closing the bedroom door and flinging on her clothes. She took a quick look in the mirror and tried to compose herself. She wanted him—that was the trouble. Living with Arturo was not as easy as she had made out to Max. She was living with temptation, and she hadn't anticipated this when she had married Arturo. She wanted him and she couldn't do anything about it. And even if he were interested in her, she wouldn't do anything about it. There was no time to ask herself the whys and wherefores of that thought, she just knew it was a wise thought.

'It's about the house,' said Arturo. 'Have you contacted any realtors?'

Taken aback, Carol sat facing him on the settee. 'Well, no. We only spoke briefly about this last week and you didn't tell me to see the estate agents. I mean, I'm not sure what it is you want.'

'I thought I'd leave that up to you. The only stipulation I'll make is that I'd rather stay on this side of La Jolla, in or near the hills. Unless you particularly want to live near the beach?'

Wanting to ask him a dozen questions all at the same time, she floundered for a moment. 'No, not at all. I love it here, the view, the—Oh, I'm really confused, you know. Your patients tell me you're so easy to talk to, but frankly I find it almost impossible!'

He looked astonished. 'What's the matter? Don't you want to move into a house? You said it would be nice to have a garden, somewhere Paul can play and——'

'Yes, yes, I know. I do. It would. But what kind of house are you thinking about? What can you afford? When can I make appointments to view? And are you sure you want to do this? Are you satisfied with the way things . . . with the status quo?'

He looked vaguely relieved. 'I see, I see. And you, Carol? Are you satisfied with the way things are going?'

She gave him a friendly smile. A friendly, deliberate smile which softened the tinge of impatience in her voice. 'Don't throw the question back at me. I'm asking you.'

It was as if he didn't know what she was fussing about. 'All right. Yes, I'm satisfied. I'd have thought that was obvious.'

'With you, nothing is obvious.'

He looked at her strangely and grunted. 'Then let me draw you a picture. We want a house that's not too big, not too small. Something with a couple of spare bedrooms, perhaps. Preferably three, but no fewer than two bathrooms. There'll be a room I can make into a study. There'll be a den for Paul—in which the TV will live. I find it a nuisance in the living room. I'd like a dining room that's a dining room and not part of the kitchen. If you can't find somewhere with a pool, then make sure the yard is big enough so we can have one put in. Money is no problem. When you've found somewhere suitable, tell me and I'll take time off to view it. If you're unsure where to find suitable realtors, get Nancy to help you. She'll be delighted. You see, it couldn't be more straightforward, could it?'

'No.' Carol shook her head in amazement. And you,

she thought, you couldn't be more complex, more mysterious if you tried. Never had she met anyone with such a gift for steering conversation. He had managed, somehow, to tell her what was wanted, to get her approval while at the same time he had avoided discussion of the real issue—the progress this newly-fledged marriage was making and how he *felt* about it.

'Right.' Arturo got to his feet, glancing at his watch as he did so. 'I've time for a quick coffee before I leave. It'll have to be the instant kind. Would you like a cup, Carol?'

Frustrated, and feeling unable to do anything about it, she nodded and followed him into the kitchen. 'Have you time for a sandwich, too? A quick one?'

'Please.'

She took cheese and tomatoes out of the fridge. 'Cheese and tomato all right?'

'Tomato,' he mocked. Her pronunciation of this word, more than any other, always seemed to amuse him. '*Tomahto* will be fine.'

Carol busied herself with the sandwich, bristling as he accidentally brushed against her in reaching for the coffee. There was a sharp edge to his voice as he apologised.

She said nothing. She could feel his eyes on her from behind and she bristled yet again, calling herself all kinds of idiot for reacting so when something like this happened.

The sudden silence was broken with words which punched the breath from her body. 'Carol, are you gay?'

The butter knife clattered to the floor and Carol made no attempt to retrieve it. She couldn't possibly have heard correctly. She just stared at him.

'Well?' he said, smiling, shrugging, quite unperturbed. 'Are you heterosexual or are you not?'

Ambivalent was hardly the word to describe her feelings. Laughter bubbled up inside her, but it never came to fruition because she was just too taken aback.

She didn't know whether to laugh or to cry. If only he knew! If only he knew how she felt about him! When she answered, of course, he wouldn't react one way or another. She was sure of that. Psychiatrists didn't, did they? They didn't judge, didn't pass opinions on such matters. They just asked their questions, arrows in the air, and watched where they landed so they could gather up information and work according to their findings. She bit her cheeks and said nothing.

'My dear Carol, it's a simple question, isn't it? So?'

'But why—how—what makes you think——'

'Because every time I'm standing at arm's length, you get jumpy. If I touch you accidentally you respond as if it were repugnant to you. Because you're a very attractive girl with an equally attractive personality and never once did Ellen make mention of a man in your life, past or present.' He droned on, his voice casual, neutral, and Carol opened her mouth and closed it again like a dumb, asthmatic fish. 'Because you're twenty-odd years old and you committed yourself to marriage with a man you knew nothing about, and you took pains to point out that the relationship would be platonic. That, when you also tell me you're a realist. I think that'll do for starters.'

She was speechless. Again she wanted to laugh her head off, but his observations just widened her eyes and left her bereft of words. She could see his point.

'Look, it doesn't matter to me one way or the other.'

'I'm well aware of that,' she said evenly, bending to retrieve the knife.

'So?'

'So I think I'd better get a clean knife. Excuse me.' She was smiling to herself. What a turn-up for the books this was! Well, why not keep him guessing?

But he didn't move a muscle. He was standing between her and the cutlery drawer looking incredibly attractive in a crisp white shirt which accentuated the darkness of his skin. There was an abnormal, momentary stillness—and then he reached for her.

Carol saw it coming, but she couldn't move. He had kissed her once before for quite the wrong reason and she honestly couldn't remember how she had reacted to that, she had been so upset about other things at the time. She promised herself, now, that she wouldn't react at all. This was just a thermometer—Arturo's curiosity had got the better of him.

Had she wanted to pull away from him, she couldn't have. Strong arms closed around her like the walls of a prison cell, her breasts pressed against the hardness of his chest as he lowered his head and kissed her. And kissed her. And kissed her.

That kiss was something totally new in Carol's experience. It wasn't like the first time he had kissed her. It was downright sensuous, an exploration, an invasion of her senses which left those senses reeling. Her lips had parted of their own volition, allowing him to taste, to probe, to *excite*. Her body responded immediately, hungrily, and it was all she could do not to put her arms around him and pull him closer, not to bury her fingers in the crisp blackness of his hair, which she had so often wanted to touch.

Her body's response, her aching need of him was frightening. She was conscious of so many things, and yet . . . and yet she couldn't really think straight. Such a contradiction, her mind and her body in battle with one another. The voice in her head was ordering her not to respond, reminding her that this kiss didn't mean a thing, that it was just his way of getting the answer to his question. If only she were being kissed by someone else, how easily she could feign lack of interest. How uninterested she would be!

The various thoughts, emotions, came together, a small implosion in her mind. She thrust herself away from him, her arm reaching out to steady her against the kitchen wall. 'Arturo——'

'It would have been easier,' he stated quietly, 'simply to answer my question.'

She was compelled to look into his eyes, although

she wanted more than anything to avoid them lest her own eyes told him of her desire. To Carol's mind it would be humiliating to let him know how much she wanted him when he didn't return that feeling. And he didn't. She could see no evidence of a response in him. Nothing at all. The ebony eyes were as cold as black ice.

But he knew how she felt—of course he knew. A firm but gentle hand reached out and took hold of her chin, moving her face just slightly to one side as he looked at her pupils, the flush on her cheeks, the gentle swelling of her lips and that pulse which was hammering, still, at the base of her throat.

His smile held no triumph, though, and his words were spoken without emotion. 'You made a good effort. But you've answered my question. My kiss was far from repugnant to you.'

Unaccountable panic gripped her, but she wasn't feeling in the least humiliated. Somehow, strange though it was, it was he who was preventing her from feeling like that. Maybe it was his detachedness, his cold-blooded attitude which, for once, she was grateful for. No, she felt not in the least foolish. Just scared. 'Arturo, please . . . don't do this. Let go of me.'

He dropped his hand immediately. 'What are you afraid of, Carol?'

'I'm not afraid of anything. You've had your fun, now leave——'

'Fun?'

'All right, all right, you've had the answer to your question.'

'Did the question offend you?'

'No, of course not. It's just—I—you . . . I'd like to remind you of your promise, that's all. Things are going so well, don't look for complications.'

His eyes were readable, momentarily. He didn't know what she meant. The silence he gave her was just another of his probing questions. God, he was a master at fishing; all due to his profession, no doubt.

Carol responded willingly, though, well aware of his tactics. 'I mean, don't rock the boat.'

He nodded shortly, unsmiling. 'I see. Is that what it would do?'

Carol flung her arms up helplessly. 'Now what are you talking about, for heaven's sake?'

He leaned against the fridge, thrust his hands into the pockets of his slacks. 'Would it be rocking the boat if I were to take you to bed and make love to you?'

She could hardly believe her ears. She might have thought he was playing a game with her, a sadistic sort of game, if her every instinct about him didn't tell her he wouldn't do that sort of thing. Good grief, from his tone of voice, he might just as well be discussing the weather!

Dumbfounded, by this question and by all that had happened in the last fifteen minutes, she answered very simply. 'Yes.'

Arturo looked over at the steam which was rising from the spout of the kettle, considering. 'Carol, I didn't make any promises to you,' he said at length, his tone troubled now. 'It was you who suggested a platonic relationship.'

'And you agreed——'

'I merely confirmed that I understood your intention,' he corrected, looking at his watch. 'Hell, I have to go. Now. Sorry about the coffee.'

'Arturo!' She almost screamed in frustration. What was he playing at? What the hell was he playing at?

He was already half way out of the kitchen. He halted abruptly at the way she shouted his name. 'Relax, Carol. For heaven's sake, what's wrong? I haven't got anything sinister planned, if that's what you're worried about. I just thought it important to point out that I didn't make any promises, that's all. See you around ten.'

And then he was gone.

In twenty minutes, she would have to go and collect Paul. Carol walked into her bedroom and spent the first three of those minutes standing, staring, like a fool, at her reflection in the mirror. Satisfied that she was wide awake, that she was real, that she had dreamt none of this, she flopped on to the side of her bed. She stuck her elbows on her knees and her face in her hands.

She tried hard to take stock. What was happening to her? It was easy enough to take stock of the external things—her new lifestyle, her new status, her work in Greenacres—all of which she enjoyed immensely. But it wasn't as easy to take stock of herself, of the way she was changing. She was changing. And that had little to do with her new life, her role as Paul's mother/sister. Arturo was effecting the change. Unwittingly, of course. But why? How? How could she let him affect her so? And was it a good thing or a bad thing?

Then she dismissed the notion. She was just as practical, as realistic and level-headed as ever. Her feet were still planted firmly on the ground and she was still as assertive as ever. . . . But she was less assertive with Arturo than she had been during her first couple of weeks with him. Or had that been aggression, then, born of despair?

That she liked him very much it was easy, now, to admit. Yet she was no closer to understanding him than she was to sprouting wings. Oh, she had thought she was closer to understanding him, earlier in the day, when Max had described him as deep water, a man whose passions ran deep.

But there were so many shades to him! There was Dr Kane, the authoritative man whose patients spoke of him or to him with such respect, such trust and in some cases, like Sandy Goldman, with such open admiration.

Then there was Uncle Art, the man who never, ever, kissed or cuddled his cousin but who would sit patiently with the boy and listen to him read. It was Uncle Art who dictated how much TV viewing the boy could do, when he must go to bed, and Paul adored him.

There was Art, the friend. Loved—no less than that—by Max Brenner. And Nancy, come to think of it.

And when the four of them were together, there was sometimes Art the colleague, who would slip right out of character and go off at a tangent talking psychiatric textbooks with Max—unless Nancy told them to shut up talking shop.

But if Carol were to ask a dozen different people to describe Arturo Kane, the man, she would get a dozen different answers and not one of them would be right, though Max would get nearest, of course.

Finally, there was Arturo, Carol's husband. And that was where the mystery became impossible. In the past hour he had professed to have thought it obvious he was satisfied with the way things were going. He had told her to find them a house.

Arturo, her husband who wasn't her husband. The man who had gone, now, to spend a few hours with his mistress. This, after what he had done to Carol just now—ascertaining that she was, indeed, attracted to him, then telling her what she had known all along, that he had no intention of doing anything about it.

If Carol hadn't had a sense of humour, she might have wept from confusion and frustration. But she did have a sense of humour; to make sure of it she winked at herself in the mirror and reminded herself, aloud, that she would cross each bridge as she came to it, take each day as it came. It was the only logical thing to do.

She got to her feet and picked up her car keys from the bedside table, a wry smile pulling at her mouth. Her sense of humour, her philosophical outlook and all the logic in the world was not cushioning her, right now, against the undeniable jealousy she was feeling at the thought of Arturo making love to another woman tonight. It had to be named as jealousy, negative emotion though it was. She had suppressed it till now. It would stay suppressed, as far as the world and Arturo were concerned.

But Carol couldn't fool herself.

Not any longer.

CHAPTER SEVEN

'LET's retire to the sunbeds,' Nancy suggested. 'This table's beginning to look like a battlefield!'

There were in fact two tables pushed together on Nancy's terrace, and the four adults and four children had just demolished a splendid breakfast-cum-lunch or, as the Americans called it, brunch. Nancy's maid was on duty, but Sunday was her cook's day off, so she had prepared everything herself.

'That was super, Nancy.' Carol struggled to her feet. 'But I've eaten too much.'

'You always do!' came the envious reply. 'And look at you— it's just not fair!'

Carol, like everyone else, was dressed in swimwear. She hadn't brought the emerald bikini but a more respectable one which was navy with little pink flowers on it. It was a glorious day and the sun was climbing higher and higher in a velvet blue sky.

'Where are you guys going?' Nancy asked of the departing children, cringing when they said they were going indoors to play table tennis. 'I don't know how they can,' she despaired, 'after eating so much!'

Max and Arturo had already sauntered over to the pool and stretched out on the group of sunbeds. Carol and Nancy did likewise, and Nancy immediately removed her bikini bra and arranged her arms and legs for maximum exposure to the sun.

Carol slipped on her sun specs. They were the mirrored sort which were very disconcerting to other people, because one couldn't tell when one was being looked at, but they gave maximum protection from the light. 'Sun-worshipper, aren't you, Nancy?' she laughed at her.

'I am a Leo,' said Nancy, by way of explanation.

123

'Speaking of which. . . .' She glanced over at the men to see whether she had their attention. She didn't. They had both closed their eyes, and if they weren't already asleep, they soon would be. 'Good company, aren't they?' she said to Carol in mock disgust. 'Carol; take your bra off or you'll end up with strap marks.'

The younger woman slipped the straps off her shoulders—which was as far as she was inclined to go.

'Take it off. Don't be so silly.'

Max opened one eye just long enough to wink at Carol. 'Bossy, isn't she? Is that another trait of the Leo female?'

'Leos aren't bossy,' Nancy answered for Carol. 'We just know what's best, that's all!' She was joking, but she looked expectantly at Carol and there followed, for Carol, a very awkward moment.

'Perhaps Carol's shy,' Arturo suggested in a voice which was nothing short of challenging. He didn't look at her; he didn't even bother to open his eyes.

In split seconds Carol had a little battle with herself. If Arturo hadn't been present, she would have been happy to sunbathe topless. After all, it was old hat to Max and Nancy. But he was present. He was also laughing at her. She unhooked her bikini and draped it over the back of her chair. The less fuss that was made of this, the less selfconscious she would feel. So much for not wearing the emerald bikini!

'Since you two are awake,' Nancy said drily, 'or rather, while you two are awake, may I please have your attention? I have an announcement to make.'

Both men looked directly at her. 'You're not pregnant?' Max joked—a remark which amused Arturo far more than it amused Nancy.

'No, dear. It's about my fortieth birthday . . .'

Carol was grateful for her sunglasses. She could hide behind them. While she appeared to be looking at Nancy, she was actually looking at Arturo, and he was looking at her now. For several seconds his eyes

roamed the length of her body and came to rest, quite
blatantly, on her naked breasts. She felt a ripple of
shock, as though he'd touched her there, but she didn't
respond with even the smallest change in her facial
expression. He looked directly at her and then his eyes
moved to Nancy.

It was so disconcerting that Carol had missed a piece
of the conversation. Nancy was saying something about
a birthday party.

'But, darling, you give house parties on the smallest
pretext, any excuse!' Max teased. 'And this is a special
occasion—and you're *not* having a party?'

'Max, I'm serious,' his wife replied. She was, too. 'I'm
depressed about it. And I don't want a whole lot of
people congratulating me on reaching this grand old age.'

'Nancy, you haven't reached it yet! Your birthday's
weeks away!'

'I know, I know. I'm just giving you an early
warning—no house party.'

Max fiddled with his beard and prodded Arturo in
the ribs. 'I can see her point, can't you, Art? I mean, the
house would be filled with pots of rejuvenating cream.
Gift-wrapped, of course.'

Very gravely, very unexpectedly Arturo took Max's
lead. 'And walking-sticks and woollen blankets.'

Carol laughed delightedly, more so when Nancy
glowered at them.

'A couple of hearing aids. . . .'

'Or one of those trumpets, like they had in the old
days.'

'A couple of wigs, perhaps, in case her hair falls
out. . . .'

'False teeth and a season ticket to the beauty
parlour——'

Nancy held up a hand. 'All right, all right! It'll
happen to you two, as well. Then see how you feel.
Although it's different for men, which is so unfair. . . .
Carol, will you stop that giggling? Whose side are you
on, anyway? Men are just coming into their prime when

they hit forty. Women feel differently about it. I am *not* having a party.'

'Then allow us,' Arturo said, quite seriously, 'to take you and Max out for a splendid dinner.'

'Oh, yes!' The idea appealed very much to Carol because she had never reciprocated Nancy's hospitality, and it bothered her. But it wasn't convenient to entertain people in the apartment, with no proper dining room.

'Done!' Nancy smiled gratefully. 'Do I get to pick the restaurant?'

'Of course.' Arturo sat up, giving her a chivalrous bow, but once again his eyes were roving over Carol.

Nancy didn't need time to think, to choose, although San Diego and La Jolla were full of really superb restaurants of all nationalities. 'The Starlight.'

'The Starlight it is.' Arturo smiled. 'I'm afraid I've forgotten the date of your birthday, yet again.'

'August fifteenth. It's a Monday. Will you be free?'

'I'll make it my business,' Arturo smiled. 'Remind me nearer the time.'

Carol felt a stab of—unhappiness? Jealousy. Monday was one of Arturo's free nights, but last Monday, the day of the fraught scene in their kitchen, he had found something more interesting to do with himself. Or rather, with his girl-friend.

She told herself to stop thinking like that. Stop it at once. After all, she had given him permission to continue his affair, hadn't she? Not that he needed it. Really, she had been so straight with him, had tried to bring it out into the open. Why couldn't he be straight with her? Why not just tell her what he was doing? Because he never told her anything, that was why. He never told her anything about himself, past or present.

'Sorry, Max, what did you say?' She hadn't heard a word and Max had been looking straight at her.

'The house you looked at this morning, on your way here. What was wrong with it? What didn't you like about it?'

'Everything.' Carol whipped off her sun-specs and pulled a face. 'It was too—too ultra-modern, too cold, if you know what I mean. It wasn't a welcoming sort of house. It had bad vibes, an unhappy atmosphere. And it was far too big for us.'

Max cocked an eyebrow at her. 'Is that all?'

'No, actually. They were asking an outrageous price for it, far more than it was worth. And I said to Arturo, I wouldn't pay that price for the place even if I were hung in diamonds.'

Max roared with laughter. 'Oh, I love it when you go super-English like that!' He slapped his friend on the shoulder. 'Isn't she just a breath of fresh air, Art? A breath of fresh air!'

Carol's eyes locked with Arturo's. How beautiful his eyes were, fringed with black lashes, so intense yet unreadable. Unreadable yet all-observant. Sometimes she felt as though he could see right inside her, could read her mind and look at her soul. This was one of those times, and Carol thanked heaven he couldn't read her mind, that that was just a fanciful idea and an unoriginal one at that.

'Well,' he said slowly, thoughtfully, 'Carol knows what she wants. Or maybe I should say she knows what she doesn't want.'

It was hardly an answer to Max's lighthearted question. Ostensibly Arturo was referring to the house she was supposed to find for them, but the remark embraced far more than that. Carol knew it, but she didn't expect Max to pick up any ambiguity.

He detected something, though. 'I've no doubt Carol will find what she wants,' he said lightly. 'You'll have to look hard, Carol, and it might take a long time.'

Carol pushed her sun-glasses on. Arturo had been referring to one thing and Max to something else. Happily, Arturo couldn't know what was behind Max's last remark. Dear Max! How very, very fond of him she'd grown. Like Arturo, Max was a good listener. Unlike Arturo, he was warm, open, responsive. He was advising her, was he not? He was telling her to be patient with Arturo, to look behind his cool veneer, that control behind which was locked his true personality. Yes, she would have to look hard, and yes, it would take a long time. Still, time was something she had plenty of.

The conversation switched to holidays and in due course everyone dozed off. Everyone except Carol. She was still thinking about time. Her days in San Francisco seemed like a long time ago. They seemed hazy, distant, despite their being an important landmark, in more ways than one, in her life.

Nancy's birthday was nearly seven weeks away. By then, Paul would be in the middle of school vacation. By then, maybe they would have found a house. By then, maybe Carol would understand her husband better. And maybe not.

Carol put her bra on again, even though Arturo was no longer awake to look at her. She had been terribly selfconscious, though she had hidden it well. It had been just a gesture on her part, a defiant gesture as well as a sort of 'When in Rome. . . .'

Life was so very different here. She hadn't been at all homesick—at least, not for places or things. She missed seeing her aunt and uncle, but she wrote to them every week. In fact she had written to a dozen people, but not all of them had replied. There was nobody in Lancashire who would miss her very much.

She looked from one sleeping person to the next. They were good people, all of them. And there was nowhere on earth she would rather be; no one with whom she would rather be. Her eyes lingered on the bronzed body of her husband—powerful, solid, as good as naked in the brief black trunks he was wearing. Deep inside her, desire stirred and mounted as it always did when she allowed herself the pleasure of looking at him.

He wasn't just handsome, he was a beautiful man. But more than anything, the sheer size of him was exciting. She had always liked big men. Was that because she was tall herself? Not really. She simply liked big men, broad men. Men who were men, and glad of it.

She laughed at herself, as she often did, and eventually drifted off to sleep—only to have a colourful, symbolic dream. She had read enough psychology to know what the symbols in her dreams meant, and when she was finally woken by Paul tugging at her arm, she found herself smiling.

Carol Palmer—Carol *Kane*—you ought to be ashamed of yourself!

Perhaps. But I'm not.

Mrs Gregory left Greenacres at the end of July. It was satisfying even for Carol, whose part in the patient's recovery had been so small, to see the woman smiling, waving, departing with her husband and two daughters who came to collect her.

As Arturo had once said, the small community which was Greenacres was a changing one. The man who never spoke, except to Max, was still there, though. So was Sandy Goldman. Poor, confused Sandy who was trying to find out who she was, to establish her own identity. She had been hooked on drugs, hard drugs, and had gone 'cold turkey' before she had been transferred to the halfway house. What a desperately hard time she must have had.

The taking of drugs was only a symptom, of course. Sandy's real problem was her movie-star mother, Madeline Gold. 'That's what you may call me— Madeline Gold's daughter.' How Sandy had exploited that fact, used her mother's money to buy her way out of difficult situations even while she hated it. The girl had run amok in bad company during the past few years, had been in trouble with the police; totally undisciplined and completely spoiled as she had been. Madeline was never home, that was the trouble. Madeline was married to her career on the screen and while she did love her daughter, one could be forgiven for thinking the opposite. Sandy was refusing to see her mother now. She was refusing all visitors, refusing to do anything but mope around Greenacres like a lost soul.

Paul was on holiday from school and was spending a lot of time at Nancy's house, simply because there was no garden for them to play in at Greenacres and the boys couldn't be allowed to roam the grounds. The apartment and its location was a very unsuitable place in which to bring up a child.

The house-hunting was proving difficult because there wasn't a great deal to look at. They had outlined a specific area to the realtors and Carol had looked at seven houses altogether, only two of which she had troubled Arturo to look at. One of them had been suitable, in fact, but it had been withdrawn from the market two days after they had viewed it, before they had committed themselves.

Strangely enough the telephone rang just as Carol was thinking about the house problem and it was the real estate agent, telling her of a place that had just come on the market, which had not yet been advertised. It sounded very interesting indeed, and she fixed an appointment to view it on the following Sunday, when Arturo would be able to go with her. No sooner had she put the phone down than it rang again. This time it was Nancy, asking Carol if she could manage the following Tuesday for the hairdressing appointment Carol had finally got round to mentioning. She and Nancy were going together, to a salon Nancy went to regularly in San Diego.

Arturo came home at six that evening. Paul was bathed, wearing his pyjamas and watching television with the bear with the bow tie. 'Uncle Art, we're going to see a new house on Sunday! It might be our house!'

'It certainly might. Well, that's good news. . . . Hello, Carol.' He dropped his briefcase on to an empty armchair and shrugged his jacket off.

'Hi. The agent phoned a couple of hours ago. Our appointment's at noon. Is that all right?'

'Fine. Is there any coffee in the pot?'

'Of course.' She got up to fetch him some coffee, answering him from the kitchen when he called out and asked her how long Paul had been watching TV. 'A couple of hours.'

She heard the short-lived argument from the kitchen.

'Okay, feller,' Arturo instructed, 'switch that box off.'

'Aw, but——'

'Aw but nothing.'

'But Mickey and me are watching this!'

'Mickey and *I*. Switch off, young man. Do you know what happens if you watch too many of these cartoons? You get to be as smart as Donald Duck. Hmph!'

Carol came back just in time to see Paul's look of puzzlement. 'But, Uncle Art, this isn't Donald Duck!'

'Paul.' It was the tone of voice which brought instant action, magically. Off went the television and out came Paul's latest reading book. He read to Arturo for a while, told him all about his day, then scampered off to bed.

He had been gone about five minutes, time enough to clean his teeth, when he came sheepishly back into the living room.

'I was just coming to tuck you up——' Carol began. This was something she never failed to do. This was her department and she made certain that Paul did not go short of kisses and cuddles. While Arturo didn't know what such things were, they came very naturally to Carol. She took hold of Paul's hand, but he made no effort to move; he was looking anxiously at his cousin.

'Uncle Art. . . .'

Arturo lowered his newspaper and raised his eyebrows. 'That's me.'

'When we do find our house, will it have a *big* yard?'

'Yes.'

'With trees?'

'Yes.' Arturo looked at Carol, both of them wondering where this was leading.

Paul began uncertainly. 'Well, could I. . . .' Suddenly

his attitude switched and he was very assertive. 'Then I can have a dog!'

Arturo didn't respond. He just looked at the boy.

'Can't I?' Paul's voice was far less certain now. 'Uncle Art?'

It seemed that Arturo would never answer him. It seemed as if minutes passed and he just went on looking at the boy. Carol wanted desperately to say something, to say yes, but she didn't dare. Both she and Paul were waiting.

Finally he nodded, very, very slowly and Carol blinked, wondering where he had just been to in his thoughts. When he spoke, finally, his voice was— strange. 'Yes, son, you may have a dog. You certainly may.'

'Er—good. Good!' Carol felt strangely disturbed. 'Come on, Paul. Let's get you into bed.'

She glanced at Arturo as they left the room. He was miles away. She put the gleeful child to bed and came back to find Arturo staring at nothing in particular. Without a word she sat down, and when he spoke, she didn't move a muscle.

'I wanted a dog when I was Paul's age. A dog, all of my own. I thought life would be all right again if I could only have a dog.'

Carol almost stopped breathing. She didn't dare to prompt him lest she shatter his reverie, lest she spoil this *revelation*.

'I got one eventually,' he went on. 'When I was eight. When I moved in with Sam.' He laughed shortly, and although Carol knew he wasn't particularly speaking to her, she felt joyous. 'We had to move house first, though. Sam and I lived in an apartment block. It was pretty smart, in a residential area, and no pets were allowed. But that didn't stop old Sam. "Yes, son," he said, "you may have a dog. We'll rent a different apartment. No, we'll rent a house with a yard——"'

He stopped so abruptly that Carol, hanging on his every word, jumped. He looked at her, then away from her, and the silence became very uncomfortable. Because Arturo was uncomfortable. His eyes were broody, darker than ever.

'I'll—I'll get dinner.' Carol left the room for his sake.

She escaped into the kitchen and stood motionless behind the closed door, her hand over her mouth. Dear God, this incident—it should be such a little thing, but it wasn't. It was so important! It was some kind of breakthrough, and she felt honoured. A little sound escaped from her, hardly more than a murmur; a sound that was a mixture of pleasure and pain. She felt ridiculously happy because her husband had told her . . . what? Just a cameo from his past. Ah, but the implications . . .

She also felt incredibly sad. Because of Arturo's story? Why did his mother leave him on Sam's doorstep? And what of his father? But of course, his father would have been dead by then.

No, it wasn't that which brought tears to Carol's eyes. They were in danger of spilling over, and she panicked. She made a pretence of moving a few pots and pans, but dinner wasn't actually ready yet. When her silly efforts did nothing to send away the threat of tears, she walked briskly through the living room to the bathroom, telling Arturo very casually that dinner would be another fifteen minutes.

He grunted, not looking up from his newspaper. Once in the privacy, the safety, of the locked bathroom, Carol leaned her head against the coolness of the mirror and allowed the tears to fall. What an idiot she was. What an idiot! She'd been married to Arturo for three months, and she couldn't say why it had happened, she couldn't say how or when. But it had. And she was only just realising it. She loved Arturo Kane. She loved him to distraction.

So what was she going to do now? What the hell was she going to do now?

'Nothing,' she whispered to her reflection. 'You just carry on. It's as simple as that.' She'd encountered one of those problems she'd told herself never to look for and she would cope simply by continuing to take each day as it came. She was a perennial optimist and philosophical with it.

So think of the positive side of things, she told herself. Think how lucky you are to be living with . . . to be married to . . . the man you love. She *was* lucky.

Wasn't she?

CHAPTER EIGHT

'So when can you move in?' Nancy asked excitedly. 'Oh, Carol, I'm so pleased for you! It's lovely that you both felt the same way about the place! And what alterations are you going to make, exactly?'

Carol smiled at her friend's enthusiasm. They were in the thick of the rush hour traffic in San Diego, on their way to the hairdresser's, and they'd been talking non-stop about the new house ever since they had left Nancy's place. The children's nanny had taken the four boys to Sea World for the day, brave lady that she was. Carol had only read about the place, but she knew there was so much to see in that marine life park—from killer whales to dolphins, from starfish to seals and otters—that it was bound to be an exhausting day out. Still, Paul would love every minute of it, she was sure of that.

'Carol, is everything all right?' Nancy asked suddenly, in the absence of Carol's response. 'I mean, you are happy about the house, aren't you?'

'Oh, yes. Yes!' She thought she had told Nancy all there was to tell. The house she and Arturo had viewed two days earlier had been perfect, and they had both felt that very strongly. Except that it needed some structural alteration. 'I've told you, it's something of a folly, a really oddly-shaped house! Oh, but it's got such atmosphere! And there isn't a great deal to do. We want to knock two of the bedrooms into one, so it can be a bedroom-cum-den for Paul. We want to have a pool built in the back garden—yard, I mean! And we want the garage extending.'

'Is that all?' Nancy grinned, taking her eyes off the road again.

'Well, it won't take long. A couple of months,

perhaps. Then we'll redecorate throughout, and Bob's your uncle.'

'What?'

Carol giggled. 'I mean, and then we can move in!'

The conversation stopped as Nancy manoeuvred her car into a parking space. 'Boy, that was lucky! Fancy finding space at this time of day! The hairdresser's just across the road from here.'

The 'hairdressers' was unlike any hairdressers Carol was familiar with. It was all mirrors, spotlights and stainless steel—and very, very swish with its plush seating and immaculately uniformed staff. Here, it appeared, one could have everything from a pedicure to a massage!

It would have been easy to spend the entire day in that establishment, but they didn't. They each had a facial and a manicure and were then handed over to a hairdresser called Pete—a short, pretty man who had blond tints in the most natural-looking perm Carol had ever seen. But it was a perm, of that she felt certain. Carol also felt certain that Pete would be good at his job, but he was unbearably extrovert!

'Mrs Brenner, it's so good to see you!' He greeted Nancy like a long-lost friend (despite the fact that she had been there the previous week). 'And Mrs Kane, welcome! Welcome! Oh, madam, we must do something about this!' He took hold of Carol's hair as though it were something disgusting, picking up a strand, then dropping it. 'This style is all wrong for you! Why, it isn't even a style!'

Carol groaned inwardly, embarrassed as a woman who was just getting up from her seat turned round and stared.

'If Madam will just sit down,' Pete said buoyantly, 'I'll be back in two minutes and I'll show you exactly the style for you!'

'Oh, my God,' Carol groaned to Nancy, 'he's going to suggest cutting my hair, I just know it! And I only want a trim——' Realising she had lost Nancy's

attention, she stopped. Nancy was giving a little wave
to the woman who had stared, who was now walking
briskly towards the cash desk.

'It's Mrs Landis, isn't it?' Nancy smiled. 'Nancy
Brenner, remember? Dr Brenner's wife. We met at the
hospital last Christmas, at the staff dance——'

'Of course.' The woman shook hands with Nancy.
'I'm sorry, Mrs Brenner, I didn't see you. I—I was just
on my way out.'

Carol felt a sudden emptiness inside her. Mrs Landis
was lying. She had seen Nancy. Furthermore, her
discomfiture was evident—to Carol if not to Nancy.
But then Carol knew the reason for that discomfiture.
This was the woman who had telephoned that first
morning. Her voice, her soft drawl, was unmistakable.
This was Arturo's lady friend. His *married* lady friend.

'Fancy seeing you here, of all places,' Nancy was
saying. 'Is it your day off?'

'Yes.' Mrs Landis smiled politely. 'This is a special
treat for me. I haven't had my hair done professionally
for more than six months.'

Naturally, Nancy made the introduction, oblivious to
any kind of atmosphere, to the fact that Mrs Landis
was uneasy. 'Mrs Landis, this is Mrs Kane, Carol
Kane. Carol, meet Sonia Landis. Sonia works at the
mental hospital.'

'How do you do?' Carol offered her hand and
responded automatically. She wasn't pleased to meet
this woman, she was merely interested to take a look at
what she was up against.

Sonia Landis was somewhere between thirty and
thirty-five. She wasn't beautiful, but she was certainly
attractive, vivacious. She was dark, tall and slim, but
not too slim. Her figure was beautifully proportioned,
rounded, even voluptuous. Oh yes, she was one of those
women who would appeal to any man; there was that
certain *something* about her. A very feminine, physical
something.

Carol let go of her hand, her eyes lingering

deliberately on the woman's wedding ring. 'Mrs Landis, you know my husband, of course?'

'Yes. I—we—work together two days a week.'

Carol looked straight into her eyes. Blue eyes. 'You see him twice a week?' She smiled, but it was an effort.

There was so much happening on the periphery. Work continued in the salon, the customers and hairdressers chatted against a background of piped music. A cash register rang in the reception area behind them and Pete, armed with a hairstyle magazine, came striding towards them.

'Mrs Brenner, take a look at this, will you? I'm sure you'll agree with me. . . .' He spoke to Nancy, not to Carol, probably because Carol and Sonia Landis were in the midst of speaking to one another.

Carol registered all of this, and the fact that her ambiguity had not gone unnoticed by Sonia Landis.

'Well, I—Yes.' Mrs Landis shifted slightly. 'And Dr Brenner, too, of course.'

'Of course,' Carol said evenly. Both Max and Arturo put in two days a week at the mental hospital. 'You're a psychiatrist, too, are you?'

'Nothing so grandiose. I'm a senior psychiatric nurse.' Guilt was written all over the woman's face, though she was doing her utmost to be casual.

How strange is human nature, Carol thought. She knows that I know. Had Nancy not been present, and ignorant of what this woman was to Arturo, Carol would have said something outright, though she had no idea quite what that would have been. As it was, she came as close as she dared to confronting the woman, not pausing to think of possible consequences. She felt as jealous as hell. 'We've spoken to one another before, actually.' It was not a question but a statement. Carol said it lightly but positively. 'On the telephone, remember?'

Mrs Landis' eyes dropped momentarily. She shook her head as if in denial, but when she spoke, she answered truthfully. 'Yes, I believe so. I—I. . . .'

'You wanted to speak to Arturo,' Carol finished for her.

'Carol——' Nancy broke in then, 'look at this magazine! It's really quite exciting. Oh, excuse me, Mrs Landis—I'm so sorry!'

Sonia Landis grasped the opportunity of getting away, muttering something about some shopping she had to do, and making her way quickly to the cash desk.

The following couple of hours were hardly more than a blur to Carol. She made a pretence of interest in the magazine Pete thrust into her hands, heard his and Nancy's enthusiasm over how much the depicted hairstyle would suit her face, but all the time her mind was on the woman she had met. Arturo's lady friend. Arturo's married lady friend.

No wonder Nancy knew nothing of Arturo's affair with her—which probably meant that Max knew nothing, either. But why should they? Arturo was a very private person, even with them, and he would have had to be discreet even before he married Carol, in view of the fact that Sonia Landis wasn't free. Which thought gave rise to another possibility, one that Carol hadn't considered before: was Arturo in love with this woman?

He might have been in love with her all along but unable to do anything about it because she wasn't free. No. No, that didn't ring true. He would hardly have married Carol if that were the case, no matter how extenuating the circumstances concerning Paul. He would have kept himself free in the hope that Sonia would divorce her husband. And if Sonia didn't want to divorce her husband . . .?

All in all it looked as if love didn't enter into this affair, which meant it was a purely sexual thing. That sounded more like it. That sounded more like Arturo. Really, it made not a great deal of difference to Carol; she couldn't have been more jealous even if Arturo were in love with the woman. He felt nothing whatever for

Carol, not even sexual attraction. It was that, that absence of any feeling whatever, which hurt more than anything.

'Pete,' Carol said at length, in the face of a lot of professional, persuasive jabber she had hardly absorbed the meaning of, 'just do as you like.' She forced herself to smile. 'You have carte blanche.'

Not only did Pete cut her hair, he also gave her a demi-wave, insisting that it would give more body to the new style. It seemed to take an age. What should have been a pleasurable morning had turned into an ordeal for Carol. But she hid it well—as was her wont.

The effervescent Pete did a masterful job on her hair. He left it fairly long and he layered it, blow-dried it so that soft feathers framed her face.

When Carol looked at the finished result, she was so staggered that Sonia Landis was temporarily pushed from her mind. She looked—really quite attractive! The new style softened the facial features she had always thought were too sharp, and her hair seemed so much thicker now, far shinier than it had been before. She was very pleased and she tipped Pete accordingly.

The total price Carol paid for all this treatment might have upset her on any other day. But not today. She was too upset, too sick to think of money today. The weeks ahead of her would be difficult. She was going through a period of adjustment. To the fact that she had fallen in love with Arturo. To the fact that he felt less than nothing for her. To the fact that he was having an affair with another woman. A married woman. Just what sort of crazy world was she living in?

'You look great!' Nancy enthused, looking pretty great herself when they left the salon. 'Carol, you're a different girl. Oh, I've had a lovely time. You know, you look gorgeous? What a difference that new hairstyle makes. I'm telling you, you're a different girl!'

Carol smiled inwardly. Indeed she was a different girl from the one Nancy had met a few months ago. But nobody would know of the internal changes. Of that she was determined.

When she collected Paul from Nancy's house, he was unable to stop looking at her, giggling and saying how nice she looked. Even Arturo remarked on her new image. That was certainly what she had these days, what with her suntan, her new style of dressing and this hairdo she hadn't wanted but was pleased with.

Unlike Paul, Arturo didn't stare or enthuse. That evening was one of his late nights. He came home around ten and blinked in surprise. Carol switched the TV off and asked if he would like a snack.

'Am I in the right apartment?' he smiled.

'Does that mean you like it, or not?' If she didn't ask, she'd probably never find out.

'You look lovely,' he said. And though he had said it casually, it was so unexpected that Carol's mouth opened and closed in surprise.

She made him a snack and she made light conversation, too. As far as he was concerned, she was unchanged beyond her physical appearance. She tried very hard, then and in the days that followed, not to think about the woman she'd met in the hairdresser's.

Arturo was still working long hours. He came home when he could for a couple of hours in the afternoon, to be with Paul. He spent as much time as possible with Paul, but it really wasn't much. He had mentioned that he was looking for a fourth doctor to join the private practice in San Diego, in an effort to lessen his workload.

Max had told Carol that Arturo had difficulty in refusing to take on new patients, not because he needed the money but because he couldn't refuse to give help. It seemed to Carol that all she knew about her husband had been learned from other people. It was Nancy who had told her that Greenacres had been bequeathed to Arturo by a grateful patient—a millionaire financier who had made no stipulation as to what Arturo should do with the mansion. Arturo had chosen to convert it into a 'much-needed' establishment, a halfway house, for his own patients and for Max's, and for those of several other doctors in the area, when there was room for them.

Carol loved him for that. After all, he could have sold Greenacres and pocketed the money or even lived in it himself, instead of living in a small apartment tagged on the back of the building. True, the patients paid handsomely for staying at Greenacres, but they could all afford it very easily. As for Arturo's poorer patients—well, he gave his time freely to them.

Perhaps he found it easier to love mankind than he did to love individuals. And yet ... and yet he loved Paul, she was sure of that. He just wasn't very good at showing it, not in a physically demonstrative way, at least.

Carol understood, now, why it had been so important to Arturo that he kept the boy with him. His reasons were not unlike her own. As Carol had wanted Paul as much for Ellen's sake as for his own, Arturo had wanted to repay a debt to his Uncle Sam. Arturo, abandoned by his widowed mother when he was eight, obviously identified with the boy and wanted to do for Paul what Sam had done for him at a similar age. This, at least, was something Carol understood about her husband. Arturo could, after all, have given Carol a financial settlement in order that she might take the boy back to England and be sure of giving him some material comfort.

She would probably never know whether Arturo would actually have gone to court over Paul. Still, the marriage was working out all right—as far as Paul was concerned. And he was the important one. It was just that for Carol things had changed recently. Loving Arturo brought with it unhappiness. She only hoped she would be able to continue to hide that unhappiness. Of course she would. She must. For Paul's sake.

It had to be the yellow dress. She hadn't worn it yet

because it was really a little too dressy for everyday wear. But it wasn't really suitable for evening wear, either.

Carol took it out of her wardrobe and looked at it. It was cocktail length, she supposed, finishing just below the knee. It had a straight skirt and plain, low-necked bodice and thin shoulder straps, no wider than laces. Which meant she couldn't wear a bra with it because she didn't possess a strapless bra.

She tried it on. They were going to the Starlight for Nancy's birthday dinner, and time was marching on. Paul was at Nancy's house already and he would be sleeping over because tonight would be a late night. Arturo had been home about five minutes and was taking a shower. They were picking Nancy and Max up at eight-thirty.

'Oh, yes,' she nodded in satisfaction. The dress was fine. 'It just needs. . . .' It just needed a little something to add a touch of glamour. Her mother's jewellery box provided the answer. Carol found a silver necklace with matching ear-rings which had been an anniversary gift from Sam. Ellen's make-up box was there too, in Carol's drawers with the other items and mementoes she had kept. A little make-up would be in order tonight. Why not? Nancy would be dressed up to the nines, no doubt, and looking perfect.

One layer of mascara and a touch of brown eye-shadow made Carol's hazel eyes seem even larger. She was pleased with the effect and added just a touch of blusher and lipstick. She popped the lipstick into her bag, slipped into her new, medium-heeled sandals and examined her reflection in the mirror. She brushed her hair, which was behaving very well thanks to the demi-wave and was no trouble at all, and she was ready. With a quick dab of the perfume she had treated herself to when buying some for Nancy's birthday gift, she went into the living room to wait for Arturo.

The perfume she had bought for Nancy was French and wildly expensive—and the biggest bottle available.

It wasn't the most original gift idea, but really, what could one buy for a woman who had everything? Carol had treated herself to a tiny bottle of something less expensive but still exotic. She couldn't seem to get used to the idea of having plenty of money, to the fact that she could buy virtually anything she wanted. Arturo was really very generous and he . . .

And he looked magnificent. He came out of his room looking relaxed and no less than stunning in black trousers, a white dinner jacket and immaculate shirt, and a black bow tie. Carol's confidence over her appearance vanished at once. She should have bought something more dressy. She got to her feet a little uncertainly, but she needn't have worried.

'You look beautiful,' he said slowly, and the way his eyes travelled over her almost convinced her that he meant it.

'Thank you. You look—pretty good yourself.' Her stomach contracted nervously. They were standing yards apart, but his presence, that very physical presence, was beckoning to her almost irresistibly.

She looked away, uneasy under his scrutiny, and picked up the beautifully wrapped bottle of perfume with hands which were trembling slightly.

It was worse when they got in the car. His nearness and that faint whiff of the tangy soap he always used affected her unreasonably. She was quiet without realising she was quiet.

Sandy Goldman was strolling along Greenacres' drive with a couple of other patients. She waved energetically as the Mercedes went past, smiling at Arturo rather wistfully.

Carol watched him from the corner of her eye as he drove the big car smoothly, effortlessly, her eyes being drawn again and again to the strong, capable hands on the wheel. For an instant she was plunged into the past, into a scene which was very hazy in her memory. She couldn't remember where they had been going to, or where they had come from, she remembered only looking at his hands and the fact that she had felt intense hatred for him at the time. And now ... now. ... Oh, what she felt for him now!

When Nancy and Max were settled in the back of the car, it was easier, the atmosphere relaxed and happy. Nancy, despite her entering a new decade, was in a very good mood and as chatty as ever. They got to the Starlight at nine and settled in the cocktail lounge to have pre-dinner drinks.

'You've never had a Margarita?' Nancy asked, shocked. 'You've been here all this time and you've never had a Margarita?'

She was referring to a cocktail which Carol had seen advertised many times but had never actually tried. This was put right at once and she found herself served with a drink in a very wide-rimmed glass, half-filled with finely crushed ice and perfectly innocent-looking.

Carol wasn't particularly keen on it at first, but by the time she was halfway through it, she had begun to like it enough to order a second.

'You'll have to watch it,' Arturo warned her, while shooting Nancy a look of mock disapproval. 'Those things are far more powerful than they appear.'

'That's right,' Max put in. 'They've got a real kick in them, Carol. You'll see what I mean when you stand up!'

The evening began and continued beautifully. Carol did feel the effect of her drinks when they walked into the restaurant, and was glad she hadn't finished the second. She needed food.

The Starlight was a gorgeous place, set on a cliffside overlooking the Pacific, the wide sweep of the bay twinkling with lights under a black, starlit sky. There was an indoor restaurant, but the four of them sat outside to eat in a sub-tropical garden setting which was romantic in the extreme. There were colourful plants everywhere, lit by hidden spotlights. The air was slightly perfumed and velvety in its warmth, and in the background there was the gentle sway of palm trees. An August evening in California; it was perfect.

There was dancing outdoors and in the restaurant under cover. A small combo was playing soft music from a tiny stage in the indoor restaurant, which was clearly visible from where they were sitting. Couples drifted on and off the dance floor, some indoors, some dancing out in the garden.

Nancy and Max danced while waiting between courses, and Carol and Arturo discussed the various dishes on the menu. There was all sorts of food available, but the Starlight specialised in seafood and, under Arturo's guidance, that was what Carol had chosen. She had started with classic style Oysters Rockefeller, and when the main course arrived, she smiled in delight at its presentation.

'It's a pleasure to watch you eat!' Max laughed as the waiter refilled the wine glasses, Arturo declining a refill.

'Carol's on a seafood diet tonight,' Nancy's laugh was gurgly, she was getting chattier as a result of the wine. 'She sees food and she eats it!'

Max groaned at the old joke, but Carol hadn't heard it before and she, too, found she was a little giggly. She made a mental note to watch her wine consumption.

'So how is it?' Arturo enquired.

'Mouthwatering!' Carol was eating Crab Imperial— delicate crabmeat in supreme sauce, baked in a mollusc shell. 'It's super, Arturo, thank you!'

Her enthusiasm brought a smile to his lips and Max looked at him fondly, smiling because Arturo was smiling.

When the course was finished, Arturo held out his hand to Nancy. 'Well, birthday girl, how about a dance?' They went indoors, dancing among half a dozen other couples to the song of a male singer who had a really good voice and a style all of his own. When the singer left the small stage and the music changed to something more lively, Arturo and Nancy danced on.

'How're things?' Max asked, watching Carol watching Arturo.

'Fine.'

'Really?'

'Really.' She looked levelly at Max. 'Honestly! Things are just fine!'

'So how come you seem to be avoiding dancing with each other?' Max probed.

'Don't be silly. You're imagining that.'

Maybe he was, maybe he wasn't. It certainly wasn't Carol's place, she felt, to ask Arturo to dance with her. She didn't want to dance with him, anyway. It was just about the last thing she wanted.

'Would you feel foolish if you were to dance with a man five inches shorter than you?' Max asked then, looking very uncertain.

'Not if you were the man concerned,' she answered honestly. No, with Max she would never feel foolish, and even so, there was no way she would risk hurting his feelings by refusing his invitation.

They danced separately, in keeping with the music, smiling over at Arturo and Nancy when they waved. It was only when the dance was finished and Arturo came over and took Carol's hand that it occurred to her that Max might not have wanted to dance with her at all, that he might have engineered this in the hope that Arturo would take over.

Arturo did take over, and unfortunately the music changed again and the dancers moved into each other's arms. Carol felt immediately uneasy as Arturo's arm came around her and he pulled her close, so close that she could feel the heat of his body. 'Relax,' he murmured, his breath a cool breeze against her temple.

She couldn't relax. She could hardly breathe for the effect he was having on her. Immediately the dance was over she walked away, almost rudely, but he took hold of her arm as she stepped out into the garden. 'Just a moment,' he said quietly, with the slightest hint of amusement in his voice. 'I want to show you the view.'

They skirted the dancers and stood at the edge of the

garden, looking out over the silent ocean and a myriad
lights, down on their right, which was La Jolla.

'La Jolla,' he said quietly. 'The Jewel.'

Carol nodded, unsure whether to say anything. Then
his arm came round her waist and while she thought he
was guiding her back to the table, he stopped on the
edge of the dancing area and took her into his arms.

'Let's try again.' He smiled, but his eyes dared her to
refuse, to walk away again. 'Perhaps you'll feel safer in
the open air.'

She didn't feel safer in the open air. It was much
darker out here, so sweetly romantic that that in itself
affected her. She became aware of her heartbeat,
accelerating. Then she became aware of Arturo's lips
brushing against the side of her temple and his
heartbeat as he held her very, very close.

Within seconds Carol's hands were trembling and she
was left in no doubt whatever that Arturo wanted her
as much as she wanted him. She tensed. 'Arturo, no!'
She would have moved away from him, but his arms
wouldn't allow it.

'Carol, please,' he said softly, in a voice which had
deepened, even roughened. 'You better stay right where
you are for the moment. Otherwise we'll have all heads
turning in our direction.'

Carol felt the blush rising from the base of her throat,
was grateful she was too close to Arturo for him to be
able to see it. She felt helpless, excited by his arousal, so
immediate, so ardent! But this was lunacy! Confusion
raged inside her. They were in a public place and she
had no choice but to stay close to him, yet if she
did. . . . She couldn't bear this—this pleasure, this
punishment, this potentially embarrassing *craziness*.

'For God's sake, Arturo, loosen your hold on me!'

'Why? Why fight it, Carol? How much longer do you
intend to fight this? Another month—two—six? You
told me you were a realist, did you not? Why not start
being realistic right now, tonight?'

She glanced round frantically, hoping no one could

hear. That was hardly likely, though. Arturo's lips were against her ear, moving slowly now along the silky skin of her throat. The ache inside her was unbearable, the urge to press herself even closer to him——

'Please, Arturo, stop it! Stop that or I'll walk off this floor. You're crazy, this is crazy! *I don't want this!*'

'Your body tells me otherwise, Carol.' He lifted his head and looked into her eyes, his smile wicked.

His arms were a steel band around her, his thighs hard and warm against her own. She had to get out of this ludicrous situation, and fast. She was scared by this, by what it might do to their relationship, by what it would do to her emotions. For him it was sex and nothing more, but for Carol it would be ... oh, so much more than that. Beyond this, beyond the flood of passion she was experiencing, the face of Sonia Landis floated into her mind. Not that the woman was ever far from her thoughts.

She had vowed never again to mention this thing to Arturo, but she had no choice but to do so now. She could not, would not, make love with Arturo when he was in the throes of an affair with someone else. Furthermore, the mention of his mistress should serve nicely to cool his ardour, and then she could make her escape from him.

'By the way,' she said quietly, feeling wicked and enjoying it, 'I forgot to tell you a couple of weeks ago, I met your mistress.' She spoke rapidly, before he had a chance to answer her, feeling him move back in surprise, putting a slight distance between their bodies. 'It was when I was in the hairdressers. Nancy introduced me to her, perfectly innocently, of course. Mrs Sonia Landis, that is—your mistress.'

'And how did you figure that out?' He spoke quickly but not in an attitude of denial.

'She has a very distinctive Southern drawl. I recognised her voice, believe it or not. There was that, plus her discomfiture when Nancy introduced us. Though Nancy didn't notice anything, as I say.'

'And you?'

'And I . . . I said nothing, don't worry.'

Arturo looked straight into her eyes, well and truly distracted. 'There should be no need for discomfiture—for anyone. My affair with Sonia was finished on my first day back at work. I told you, that night.'

He hadn't, actually. He had just told her to forget it, not to worry about it. But she had worried. She had worried ad nauseam since she realised how much she loved him.

Carol's ploy had worked beautifully. And she didn't regret what she had done, said. In fact, her heart had lightened considerably because he had said his affair with Sonia was finished, had been finished since that first night. Was he lying? She thought not. Arturo was the sort of man who would remain silent rather than lie, she felt sure of that. But he was still seeing Sonia. In the course of his work he saw her, there was the temptation of her two days a week. . . .

He was guiding her back to the table, the dark eyes watching her as they walked. She wondered whether he was angry with her, angry in that ever-so-quiet way of his. Then she saw amusement in the ebony eyes and he laughed shortly as they sat down, amused by some thought she might never know about.

'What's the joke?' Max asked the question as they sat down, but Arturo shook his head and signalled the waiter. Coffee was served, brandy was served, and the evening wore on.

The scene on the dance floor had had a sobering effect on Carol and she felt tense, needing to make a deliberate effort to appear natural and relaxed during the remainder of the evening. Several times she looked up to find Arturo watching her, the black eyes almost sensual. She looked away quickly when this happened, acutely aware of the tension crackling between them, sexual tension.

When they took their guests home, Carol accepted their offer of coffee before Arturo had a chance to refuse. They stayed at Max's house for almost an hour, but she couldn't delay going home for ever.

Nothing was said on their short drive home. Carol made a pretence of looking out of the car window, her heart beating a tattoo against her ribs. The air was charged with sensuality, inevitability.

Arturo reached for her as soon as they got inside the apartment and Carol yielded to his kiss without so much as a protest. He had been distracted only temporarily by mention of Sonia Landis and had been amused by Carol's ploy. Amused and not in the least put off.

'Why fight it?' he had said, and she had known, then, she would be powerless to resist if he pursued her in private. She had known weeks—months—ago that she would not be able to resist him. She had known also that she must have no delusions over what it meant. She reminded herself of that even as she willingly succumbed to his lovemaking. And then, suddenly, she became incapable of rational thought. . . .

His lips moved over her throat, her shoulders, as the straps of her dress were slipped aside and his fingers slid open the zip. She stepped out of her dress, her breasts naked, pert, hungry for his touch as he shrugged out of his jacket and picked her up effortlessly.

He laid her down on her bed, his lips seeking her taut nipples and sucking, taunting, kissing until she reached for him in a frenzy, helping him to shed his clothes. Her hands slid over his chest, pale against the darkness of his skin; the masculine smell of him, the feel of him intoxicating her as she slipped into a vortex of raw desire.

And then his mouth was on hers, probing erotically before returning yet again to her breasts. She arched against him, her hands exploring every inch of that hard, muscular body, his arousal inflaming her further.

Not a word was spoken. There was only the sound of his breathing, quickening, ragged, as his lips moved over the soft swell of her stomach, and then there was her gasp of pleasure at the sweet ecstasy which was his most intimate exploration of her.

She moaned breathlessly into the semi-darkness as he moved over her, her hands locked on to his hips, pulling him closer as one powerful thigh parted her legs. Then their bodies were entwined as they became one and beyond the emotional, the spiritual gratification, there was a short, sharp physical pain which sent the breath rushing from Carol's lungs and made her arms stiffen against his back in momentary rejection.

Arturo withdrew at once, cursing softly as he turned his head sharply away from her. Carol's breathing was audible in the room and she reached out for him, bereft at his withdrawal. With a groan, his lips found hers and his lovemaking suddenly changed dramatically. Gone was the fierce ardour of his earlier kisses. He kissed her now as if her lips were sweet wine to be savoured, tasted slowly, and his hands became gentle as he caressed her body. Never would she have believed he was capable of such tenderness. Carol sighed deeply, her body fluid beneath his intimate caresses. Her skin, her nerves, every fibre of her being became more and more sensitised until she could bear no longer the hunger, the yearning inside her. She stilled his hands, those strong, gentle hands of the man who knew more about her body than she would ever have dreamt he could know. Just once she spoke his name and then they were joined once again in that ultimate embrace.

The rhythm of his lovemaking was slow, almost cautious, and all the more erotic to her because of it. She cried out to him, her mouth seeking his until they were kissing in a frenzy and their passion, their need, swelled and mounted until once again all gentleness was abandoned and all hunger and need was slaked.

How long they had lain in silence, Carol had no way of knowing. A quarter of an hour, half an hour, two hours—whatever. Time seemed to be standing still. The silence of the room was so loud that it disturbed her.

They were not touching, not sleeping. She was deep in her own thoughts, and Arturo ... she wondered where he had gone to while he was lying beside her.

She looked at the dark drapes which were drawn against the night, against the stillness outside. At length, his silence hurt her and she closed her eyes against the threat of tears. If he had held her in his arms, if he had even taken hold of her hand she might not have felt so deperately lonely.

'You should have told me,' he said quietly, without emotion.

'Perhaps.'

There was a single lamp giving off a soft, golden glow and casting mysterious shadows in the corners of the room.

'It was inevitable, Carol, you must have known that. If not from the start, then at some point. ... Take a lovely young woman and a man of my age and put them together in——'

'It doesn't matter.' She had no idea whether he was apologising. She hoped not. It would only deepen the hurt. If he would just reach for her, just touch her in the smallest, most casual way. ... Take a lovely young woman—how cold, how mathematical! Take one man and one woman. ...

She swallowed against the lump in her throat and said, very bravely, very casually, 'When I was twenty I vowed I would lose my virginity by the time I reached twenty-one. I don't regret this, Arturo. Not in the least.'

'So what went wrong?' There was a smile in his voice. 'I can't imagine you'd have had a problem.'

Carol looked up at the ceiling, unblinking. Was this the difference in mentality between the sexes or could he begin to understand, if she told him? Not that she had any intention of telling him. To explain to him would be to tell him she'd never loved a man before. Oh, she had been in love once ... twice ... briefly. But she had never loved someone deeply, irrevocably, the way she loved him. With him it was so different; she was more than in love with him. Much more.

And what else would she not tell him? How she had
never wanted a man the way she wanted him? How she
had never been excited, aroused to a state which had
hitherto been beyond her comprehension?

Take one man and one woman. . . . He thought it was
as simple as that! She closed her eyes tightly then, her
fingers curling into fists. She wanted to hit out at him
for the coldness of his attitude, for that mind of his
which worked so very differently from hers. The ache in
her heart became a pain as she realised how he
categorised what had happened between them. How
little it meant to him! Oh, God, how very little it meant
to him!

She thought of Sonia Landis and she believed, now,
that Arturo's affair with her was over. Dear God, she
wished it weren't. She actually wished it weren't! She
felt used, abused.

She forced herself to smile so he would hear it in her
voice. 'This was inevitable, as you say.' She even
managed to laugh a little. 'I suppose it was easier for
me, resisting all this time. I mean, they say you don't
miss what you've never had, don't they? It must have
been more difficult for you, though, since you finished
with Sonia.'

There was the movement of his head on the pillow
and Carol felt his eyes touching her face. 'What's that
supposed to mean?'

'Well,' she shrugged, turning away from him, 'you
keep telling me to be realistic.' She bit hard into her lip
in an effort to keep her voice steady. 'From now on, I
will be. I must bear in mind that your appetites go
beyond the need for food and a well-kept home.'

Arturo said nothing. But she could feel his eyes
upon her, could feel him shifting his weight on to an
elbow. 'Is that what you think?' he asked at last, his
voice as cold as ice. 'That you have to cater to my
desires, all my desires? That you're *obliged* to cater to
them?'

Carol couldn't answer. Her lashes were wet with tears and she didn't trust herself to speak. She was only grateful that he couldn't see her face.

She heard him swear, more violently than he had ever sworn before, and yet she knew only a perverse sense of pleasure, or relief, that she had succeeded in hitting back at him.

But when next he spoke, she regretted what she had said. His voice, his tone, was frightening in its coldness. 'Forget that! Get that out of your head right now! I am a slave to nothing and no one. Not to my emotions, not even to my natural—*appetites*.' He spat out the last word as if it were poison in his mouth.

Carol felt the bed give as his weight was removed from it and she turned quickly, 'Arturo——'

But he had gone. There was only the slight echo of the door closing as he left her room. She did not go after him. If she went after him she would bare her soul, let him know how much he had hurt her. And that would mean letting him know how much she cared.

If he knew how much she cared, how much she loved him, everything would surely be spoiled. He would think her a fool. After all, loving him had not been part of their arrangement.

She turned her face into the pillow and cried.

CHAPTER NINE

THE days ticked by quite normally. If Carol had angered Arturo, he didn't show it. The only difference now was that he spent even less time at home. He told Carol that he was writing a paper on a particular aspect of psychiatry, which he was presenting at a big seminar due to take place in Los Angeles in November.

Arturo had, she had learned, written several other papers on psychiatry, and she didn't doubt that some of the extra hours he was spending in his office were taken up by his current paper. But how long did it take to write such a thing? Carol lived with the knowledge that he saw Sonia Landis in the course of his work, but she didn't allow herself to dwell on the possibility, the probability, that he was now seeing her again in a very different context. If she had allowed herself to dwell on that, she would have stopped functioning.

He kept his distance from her, physically and, of course, emotionally. Not that that was anything new. But that invisible, defensive wall behind which he lived grew more impenetrable than ever. Oh, they conversed just as they always had, and when Arturo was with Paul, he was the same as ever, interested in the boy, patient with him, firm when necessary.

In the middle of September the vendors of the house they were buying vacated. Carol was kept very busy indeed, and was glad of it. There was a lot of shopping to be done, a great deal to organise. She consulted Arturo over the business of the pool they were having built in the garden, she showed him the estimates from various builders for the internal alterations they wanted doing. All of this was well under way by the first week of October, but everything else was left to her.

Whether he was simply uninterested in shopping for carpets, curtains, furniture and the like, or whether he genuinely didn't have time, she couldn't be sure. She couldn't be sure of anything with Arturo Kane. But she carried on regardless, saw to it all. Luckily she was aware of Arturo's taste from the way he had decorated and furnished the apartment. Apart from the absence of one or two touches of warmth and cosiness, Carol had liked the apartment the moment she saw it. She, too, didn't care for fuss and frills as far as décor was concerned. So she shopped for the new house—sometimes with Nancy and sometimes alone—and hoped that Arturo would approve.

They were in the fortunate position of not being in a chain as far as the removal date was concerned; they could leave the apartment whenever they wished, and Carol decided that would not be until everything was finished in the house. Fall had arrived; Paul was back at school, the weather was by no means as warm as the summer months had been, so the absence of somewhere for Paul to play was less important.

She surprised herself, really, by the meticulous care she took in buying things for the new house. In the face of Arturo's lack of interest, and she suspected that that was what it was more than a genuine lack of time, she might easily have chosen things without a great deal of thought. But she didn't, even though she paused once to wonder how long she would actually be living in the new house. Just once she wondered about that, then immediately thrust the question from her mind with something approaching shame. What right had she to expect life to be perfect? It couldn't be; it never was. She must look around her, count her blessings. She had Paul, she had friends, she had money. She had her work in Greenacres and a husband who did, at least, come home every night. All these things added up to richness, did they not?

Apart from that, she also had her strength. Inner strength. Nobody knew that anything in the Kane household was amiss. Nothing in the Kane household *was* amiss in any practical sense—not until the middle of October, when Paul quite suddenly became rather difficult to handle. It was nothing dire, just a certain amount of awkwardness on Paul's part, like getting pernickety over his food, asking the same question two or three times, complaining when bathtime came around.

Carol wondered whether she'd done something wrong, whether her attitude towards Paul had changed in some way. She thought about it and was satisfied that this wasn't the case. She adored Paul, loved him more than ever, and she played with him, gave him as much of her time as she always had. Anything she had to do, be it her work in Greenacres, her shopping or whatever, was done while Paul was in school. He was in no way neglected or ignored.

But one night she really lost her temper with him for using umpteen delaying tactics in an effort to avoid going to bed. It was a Friday evening towards the end of October and Arturo wasn't home because this was the night he lectured. Friday was the night he lectured, she didn't have to wonder whether he was with Sonia Landis. She didn't have that as an excuse for losing her temper with Paul.

He went to bed in a flood of tears, and though they hadn't been crocodile tears, he was asleep when Carol went to check on him half an hour later. She almost laughed when she went into his bedroom and found him fast asleep—Mickey lying face down beside him. But she didn't laugh, she cried.

She cried disproportionately, unreasonably, and though she tried very hard to pull herself together, the tears were still flowing when Arturo came home.

Oblivious as he was to anything else which might be wrong with her, even he couldn't ignore her tears. Not then. 'What's wrong?' He dropped his briefcase on the chair and came over to her immediately. He didn't touch her in any way.

She told him of the incident with Paul, feeling guilty and then silly because she had reacted by giving way to tears. 'He said he wanted to wait up for you,' she finished, finally getting control of herself. 'Which was ridiculous, even though it is Saturday tomorrow. He's too young to stay up so late.'

'Quite,' Arturo nodded, thoughtful. 'I'll have words with him this weekend.'

'No,' she said quickly, getting to her feet, 'don't do that. I'm sure it's just a phase he's going through. Maybe he's missing you, Arturo. Have you got something planned for Sunday? Are you taking him out?'

'Yes, of course.' He looked up at her. 'Don't bother with a snack, Carol. I had quite a good meal at the hospital tonight—for a change.'

She smiled thinly. 'How about coffee, then?'

'How about a brandy?'

'Even better.' Carol saw to the drinks, needing the distraction of something to do. 'Do you—do you think there might be something wrong at school? Paul hasn't said anything, but——'

'No harm in checking. You could have a word with the teachers, see whether they've noticed any change in him.'

She nodded, handing him his drink. Then silence reigned—an awkward, horrible silence. It was as if they had nothing to say to one another now the subject of Paul was finished with.

'Did you go——'

'I had a phone call——'

They laughed, the awkwardness momentarily eased. 'Go on,' Arturo said.

'I had a phone call from my Uncle George today.'

'And?' He stuck his feet on the coffee table. Carol had sat opposite him, uneasy if they shared the same settee. 'Has the British property market finally perked up a little?'

'It seems so. At least, as far as my flat's concerned.'

Carol's car had been sold long since, but there had been very little interest shown in her flat because, as Uncle George. had said in his letters, people just weren't buying at the moment. 'He's—we've—had an offer. It's a thousand pounds less than I was expecting, though. So I told him I'd think about it and ring him back tomorrow.'

Arturo looked at her quickly. 'Why? I mean, would a thousand pounds make that much difference to you? Now you've got a firm offer, why . . . why do you need to think about selling?'

It sounded like a loaded question to Carol. She knew a fleeting sensation of defeat before telling herself she was imagining things. 'I didn't, actually. That is—I mean, hardly. I called him back an hour later and told him to go ahead.'

He considered her. Her or what she had said, she couldn't be sure which. 'What were you going to ask me?' She asked at length.

'Whether you'd been to the house today. They were supposed to lay the carpets today, weren't they?' He got up and refilled their glasses. 'This morning, I think you said.'

'That's right. The carpets are down. They made a very good job of them, too. They look super.'

'So what else remains to be done?'

'Very little. Once the new furniture's delivered we can move in.'

He was stretched out on the settee now, his tie was loosened and he appeared to be relaxed. But he wasn't. He looked tired, too. Carol had noticed that about him lately. 'Carol, have you remembered that I'll be away during the second week of November? The seminar in L.A.'

'Yes. I—as a matter of fact I was thinking of moving during that week. I thought it would be nice for you to come home to . . . I thought I could take the opportunity of getting everything straight while you're away.'

'Won't you need some help? My help?'

'Not really. The removal men will do the bulk of the work and we haven't much to pack.'

It was settled. Carol went into the bathroom first and made her way to bed. She closed the door behind her and leaned heavily against it. The strain, the tension between them was getting worse with every passing day.

The hurt, the bitterness she had felt towards her husband on the night they had made love had long since dissipated. She had felt certain, she still felt certain, that he had turned to her for the fulfilment he was no longer getting from Sonia. But she was no longer angry about it. She just wished—oh, how she wished—she had handled things differently. If she had kept quiet they would no doubt have continued to be lovers and that might, in time, have brought them closer together as far as day to day living was concerned.

She had thought about this so many times and she had relived their lovemaking over and over again. Sometimes, her need of Arturo was so strong that it was a physical ache inside her. Even tonight, beyond the awkwardness of their conversation, she had been thinking about their lovemaking. Then, at a physical level at least, they had communicated absolutely ... Words had not been necessary.

For a long time, Carol lay awake. She was still trying to look on the positive side of things, but it wasn't so easy these days. The positive things seemed to be getting fewer and fewer, in spite of the lovely home she was about to move in to.

As ever, Arturo was the subject of her thoughts as she drifted off to sleep just as he was the first thing she thought of on waking. She woke up feeling tired, as if her sleep had done her no good at all. Her head was aching, too. A glance at her bedside clock told her it was only six o'clock. She usually slept till eight on Saturdays. She switched off the alarm which hadn't had a chance to ring and went into the bathroom in search of a couple of tablets for her headache.

Half an hour later she was strolling round
Greenacres' beautiful grounds, enjoying the early
morning air, the dew on the grass and the sight of the
trees against the pale blue of the sky. She didn't have to
worry about Paul, because Arturo was with him. He
always left fairly late on Saturdays. Most of Saturday
was taken up by his paperwork. Or so he said.

'Good morning . . . Melancholy Lady.'

Carol looked sharply around her. She wasn't startled,
just puzzled about the voice. She'd seen no one else
around this morning. 'Oh! Mr Reeve! I—I didn't see
you. You're out early.'

It was the man she had always thought of as the man
who never spoke, who spent all of his day reading. But
he had spoken to her recently, briefly, to ask her if
she'd be good enough to buy some pens for him one
day when she was going into town. Carol did little
things like that for the patients. Mr Reeve had also
started taking phone calls. Mr Reeve was making
progress.

He was sitting on a bench just a few yards away, but
Carol simply hadn't seen him. In his hands there was
the inevitable book, but he didn't resume his reading.
He was watching Carol, seemingly very interested.

She strolled over to him. 'It's a little cold to sit
outside reading, isn't it?'

He nodded and shrugged with a smile which reached
his eyes.

Carol looked at him curiously and laughed. She
didn't know what had ailed this man, she knew nothing
about him except that he was a musician, a violinist.
Max had told her that much. 'Why—why did you call
me that? Melancholy Lady?'

His hand came up to rake through his hair, greying
hair which was a little wild. 'Because that's how you
strike me, as melancholic.'

Either Carol's guard was down this morning or this
man was acutely observant. He had summed up her
mood precisely. 'I couldn't sleep,' she said lightly. 'You

know we're moving out of the apartment shortly, I suppose? It's giving me a lot to think about!'

He didn't answer, but it wasn't necessary really. All the patients knew. It was no secret. 'Oh, I don't mean just today, Mrs. Kane. That's how you've always struck me. From the first day I saw you.'

Carol pulled a face, a sort of you've-got-me-puzzled face. She didn't question him further. Even if he weren't a patient, she wouldn't have questioned him further about his impressions. After a respectable length of time, which was an easy, comfortable silence, she said something about going to start breakfast.

'Sorry,' he said quietly.

'For what?'

'For invading your private space.'

Carol walked away, smiling wryly at his choice of words. A curious man, Mr Reeve. She hoped nobody else could see what he had seen. Was her unhappiness starting to show? If so, she was slipping. She really must make an effort to get back to normal.

What was normal, exactly?

Mrs Polowski, Carol's cleaner, helped with the packing. Carol was astonished by how much there was to do, actually. Looking round the apartment she had thought there was so little—until she actually started putting things into packing cases! And it wasn't as if she were a hoarder! She wasn't one of those people who kept things and stored them away, thinking they would come in handy one day. There was more bed linen than she had realised, more crockery, more pots and pans than she had ever used. Paul had his fair share of stuff, too. Somehow, between herself and Nancy and Arturo, his store of toys had increased unbelievably since they had first come to La Jolla.

Everything was ready in time, however. Arturo was going to Los Angeles on the Monday of the second week in November and would be away all week. He was leaving in the early hours because he was driving there, and Carol tried to keep the chaos of the apartment to the minimum. She had booked the removal van for the same afternoon. With luck, she would have everything in order in the new house by the time he came home.

Then, on the Sunday night—or the early hours of Monday morning—there was an emergency in Greenacres—the first in Carol's experience. The telephone rang at a little after two a.m. and Carol heard it immediately it started ringing. She was in a sort of half-sleep, making a mental list of last-minute jobs she would have to do in the morning. She snatched up the telephone, not wanting Arturo to be disturbed. There was an extension in both their bedrooms, but she had beaten him to it.

It was Kay Sharpe. Carol listened, nodding as if the woman could see her, then hung up and went instantly to waken Arturo. He was sprawled, massive and magnificent on the bed, uncovered and as naked as the day he was born. She touched him only lightly on the shoulder and he was awake at once—yet he hadn't heard the phone. 'Kay's just telephoned. You're needed downstairs.' Carol let no alarm enter into her voice, but she was terribly upset. 'Sandy Goldman's swallowed a handful of sleeping tablets.'

'*What?* How——'

'She broke into the drugs cabinet.'

He was already off the bed. 'Goddammit! How in the hell did that happen?'

'I don't know——'

He cursed volubly, and Carol shuddered. Dear Lord, she wouldn't like to be on the receiving end of his wrath! He was absolutely furious. A certain quantity of drugs were kept in Greenacres—in a locked cabinet in a locked office. Kay Sharpe's office. Kay lived on the premises and she alone had the keys, unless she was away. Apart from that, there was always a member of staff on duty through the night.

Carol knew the anger Arturo was capable of. She had glimpsed it once. She watched him as he flung on his clothes, feeling helpless. 'There's an ambulance on its way, Arturo.'

She needn't have worried. He answered her quite calmly. The reins were firmly in place again. She only wished they would slip more often, though not in anger.

'Can I do anything, Arturo?'

He was himself again. He even seemed to think about it for a moment. 'No, I don't think so, thanks. You better get some sleep.' The last sentence was said over his shoulder as he dashed from the apartment.

Carol's eyes travelled worriedly around the room, unseeing. Sandy. Poor Sandy! What on earth had possessed her to do this?

She went into the kitchen and filled the kettle, thinking, irrelevantly, of how the Americans always teased the English about their reliance on tea at moments such as this. She drank three cups of it, and waited. And waited.

Arturo came in just before five. He was due to leave for L.A. at six. He sank into a chair at the kitchen table, not surprised that Carol had waited up for news. 'How is she?'

'She's all right.' He rubbed his hands across his whiskers. 'Her stomach was pumped and—it was just routine.'

Carol looked closely at his face. His last words were spoken strangely, impatiently. Things such as this couldn't be shocking to Arturo. Incidents like this were a part of his work. He couldn't hope to win them all; no psychiatrist, doctor or surgeon could hope to do that. 'And Sandy's mother? Did you manage to contact her?'

'No problem. Madeline's been staying at her beach house here in La Jolla each weekend.'

Carol hadn't realised this. She had thought Madeline Goldman was at her home in Beverly Hills, Los Angeles. So Sandy had been refusing to see her mother even knowing she was down here every weekend.

'Madeline's been told, but I advised her not to go to the hospital.'

Carol nodded. Sandy wouldn't want her mother with her. Her mother would be the last person she'd want.

For once Arturo's emotions were obvious. He was deeply upset and, Carol suspected, still angry. 'Did you find out how she managed to get into the drugs cabinet?'

'Oh, yes. It was quite simple! She just picked the locks. *Would you credit that?* A fifteen-year-old girl who knows how to pick locks! Dear God——'

'She's only fifteen . . .?' She broke off. It was only just dawning on her that Arturo's anger was aimed at Sandy. 'Arturo, why . . . you must realise this wasn't a serious attempt at suicide. Sandy couldn't have hoped to get away with it in Greenacres. She was bound to be discovered, to be found. It's just a cry for help. More help. Surely you must know that?'

'Of course I know that.'

Carol stared at him. There was something here which didn't add up, something which just didn't make sense. He was looking at the cup of coffee she'd put in front of him, his eyes as black as night and broody, miles away. 'It's Madeline I'm sorry for,' he said at length, his voice so quiet it was as if he were speaking to himself. 'That kid will never know how a relative feels when. . . . But I know. When Tessa——'

The name Tessa snapped him out of it. He grimaced, his eyes filled with pain. It was clear he regretted this slip, would have bitten his tongue out if he could.

Carol seized on it. This was very, very important. For her. For them. She knew that as surely as she knew she felt scared. 'Tessa? Tessa is . . . was . . . your first wife?'

For a moment she thought he was going to strike her. Anger, or *something*, blazed in his eyes and then, suddenly, it switched off. He didn't answer.

He didn't need to.

She'd shot an arrow in the air and it had touched on some sore, secret place deep inside him. 'Sam once mentioned you'd been married before,' she said softly, having no qualms whatever for telling the lie. 'She—

Tessa—committed suicide?' No wonder Sam had never mentioned her!

Arturo pushed his coffee cup away and got up so forcefully that his chair clattered to the floor, the sound of it echoing round the kitchen in the stillness of the night. 'I'll take a shower. I have to leave in forty minutes.'

Carol didn't move for the moment. She couldn't have prevented him leaving even if she'd wanted to. She didn't want to. Her heart was racing with fear, a fear she couldn't really understand. After a couple of minutes she went into her bedroom. The apartment was silent. At least Arturo's case was already packed. Tidy and methodical as he was, he had done that hours ago and all his papers were in his briefcase.

She sat on the bed and waited. She must give him time to shower and give herself time to collect her thoughts. Her heartbeat levelled off, but the sense of fear was still with her, her mind tumbling with ideas, speculations.

It wasn't until she heard the low rumble of a car engine being started that she realised he hadn't taken a shower, he'd gone! She raced through the apartment and stopped at the top of the outside staircase, watching the tail lights of the Mercedes fading from view.

She let out a cry of pure frustration and clamped her hand over her mouth. He'd left—for a week! Without so much as a goodbye. And there was so much, so much she wanted to say to him.

'Goodbye, my darling,' she murmured into the darkness. 'Drive carefully. Phone me. I love you—I love you so much.'

Would she, if she could, have said those things? Arturo had done this, left like this, deliberately. Carol went back indoors, shivering against the chill of the November air. She closed the apartment door, closed her eyes, thinking of something Mr Reeve had said to her ... something about invading a person's private space. Surely, surely she had a right to do this with Arturo? Surely she had the right, some day, to get to know the man she had married over six months ago?

CHAPTER TEN

'MAX! Come in, come in!' Carol was up to the eyes in it, but she would always have time for Max Brenner. 'Here, let me move those books so you can sit down. It's lovely to see you! I—I'll put the kettle on.'

'Morning tea?' Max sat, looking around the chaos which would be the living room once everything was cleared away and the furniture had been arranged properly.

'Morning coffee. Less of the sarcasm! Would you like something to eat?'

'Anything that's going. A piece of cake wouldn't go amiss, if you can manage that.' He patted his too-rounded stomach. 'A small piece.'

Carol made instant coffee and served it, and the cake, from a cardboard box. She hadn't unpacked her trays yet. Most of the unpacking had been done, of the new things which had been delivered and the stuff they had brought from the apartment. It was Wednesday. Arturo had been gone two days. He had phoned on the Monday afternoon, at five, and had a word with herself and Paul, but he hadn't phoned on Tuesday and his phone call on Monday, she felt sure, had been more for Paul's benefit than her own.

'We've seen very little of you lately,' Max said casually.

Carol felt guilty. 'Well, you—you can imagine how busy I've been. And Nancy's coming tomorrow, to give me a hand. She would have come today but she had a golf match arranged, or something.'

'All right,' Max smiled, '*I've* seen little of you lately. You were in Greenacres every day last week and you didn't stop by my office and have coffee with me once.'

She bit her lip. It wasn't like Max to put someone on the spot like this.

'Guilty?' The warm brown eyes crinkled at the corners.

'Guilty.'

'What's wrong, Carol?'

She started to say what she always said, but her voice trailed off in mid-sentence. 'Nothing. Everything's fine, really! I just. . . .' She couldn't say any more for the constriction in her throat. She looked down at the pale green pile of the carpet.

Max sat quietly, drinking his coffee and giving her time to compose herself. Only when she forced herself to meet his eyes did he speak. 'Carol, Arturo looks shattered these days, as if he doesn't know what sleep is. You're a ghost of your former self and I've heard from Nancy that Paul's been playing you up a lot lately. Now, are you still going to insist that everything's fine?'

'Paul's—Paul's not been getting on too well at school since he went back after the holidays. He—I think that's what's bothering him.'

'Nonsense.' He said it gently but firmly. 'You know, and I know, and Arturo knows that that's rubbish. Paul—children—are very sensitive to atmospheres in the home. You don't need me to tell you that.'

In the ensuing silence the tears started to slide, silently, down Carol's cheeks. Her coffee cup rattled on its saucer and she put it on the floor, fumbling in the pocket of her overall for a hanky.

Max came over to her and put a large white handkerchief in her hand. 'Blow,' he said, 'but don't try and stop the tears.' When he put his arms around her, the dam broke and she sobbed on his shoulder.

'Well?'

'It—I—It's all tied up with his first wife, isn't it?' She looked at him helplessly. 'That's why he's so—Oh, I don't know!'

'He's told you about Tessa?' Max sounded surprised, pleased. 'When? What did he tell you?'

'He—he mentioned her by accident, really. After he'd sorted out the Sandy Goldman business.'

'Is that all? He just mentioned her name—or what?'

'Just her name. In the circumstances, the way it came out and the timing and everything, I—I just guessed what Tessa had done.'

'And?'

'And he slammed out of the room, saying he was going to take a shower. The next thing I knew, he'd started his car and left for the seminar. Oh, Max, why didn't you tell me? All this time—why didn't you tell me?'

He looked at her gravely, apologetically, and moved away, pacing the floor. 'Because I didn't think that was the wisest thing to do. For you. For Art. For you as a couple. I wanted it to come from him—it still has to. Do you understand that?'

'A couple? A couple! Max, we've never been a couple. We were two crazy people who entered into a stupid marriage——'

'For a very good reason. But yes,' he smiled, 'it was a crazy thing to do. Paul was only five years old. You both realised you'd have to stay married for a long time. And you weren't in love with Art when you married him, were you?'

'No.' She laughed hollowly. 'I was—merely intrigued by him. I wasn't even sure that I liked him.'

Max let out a long breath. 'Carol, I'm interfering——'

'Yes,' she said quickly. 'Please carry on, Max. If this is interference, then carry on.'

'You must talk to him, Carol. You must.'

'I can't!' she cried. 'Oh, you don't know what it's like, what he's like! I can't get near him.' Especially since the night I managed to do just that, she added to herself.

'I hope that one day you'll realise how much he needs your love, Carol. He married you——'

'Max, we've just discussed the reason for our marriage. You've known the reason all along. Well ... perhaps you didn't know quite how we rowed over Paul, that we got to the stage when we were talking of thrashing it out legally. I don't know whether Arturo actually told you that. It doesn't really matter. I don't know whether he'd actually have gone to court, had it come to that. I don't know whether I would, either. Looking back, there was a certain amount of bluff on both sides. We were both afraid we'd lose, so we married to eliminate that risk.'

'He would. Have gone to court, I mean.' Max shook his head sadly. 'He'd have fought you to the end. But he didn't, Carol, he married you!' He held up a hand as she started to protest. 'Look, Arturo must have seen something in you, felt something for you. He must have known your marriage could work out. Whatever he isn't, you can take it from me that he's an excellent judge of character. He *knows* people.'

It wasn't much to cling to. It was something, but not much. 'Has he always been like this, Max? So bloody, unbearably aloof?'

'Ah. . . .' Max sat down again, seemingly stuck for words. For a moment he went off into his own thoughts, his smile wry. 'No. If you'd known him in the old days, you wouldn't recognise him now.'

'The old days?' Carol's stomach shifted sickeningly. 'Before Tessa?'

'Before Tessa.'

'Max, please explain——'

'Talk to him, Carol. About this. It must come from *him*, don't you see that? He's given you an opening. He's mentioned her. There's a chink in his armour at last—thank God. And tell him how you feel.'

'Max, I——'

'Tell him!' He got up, looking at his watch. 'My dear Carol, I have to go.' He walked to the door and turned to find her staring at him, lost, bewildered. 'Take my advice, Carol. Act upon it.'

And then he was gone.

Carol moved around like a zombie, doing things mechanically. For the rest of that day she thought things over until she was dizzy with it. She neglected

nothing, neither the work in the house nor Paul. When
Arturo phoned she asked all the right questions about
the progress of the seminar, how his paper, his speech,
had been received. But she couldn't talk to him over the
phone.

She doubted whether she'd be able to talk to him at
all.

Nancy said nothing to her on Thursday and Carol
was grateful for that. Whether Nancy knew that Max
had visited, Carol couldn't be sure. But she would have
learned nothing more from Nancy in any case.

Carol needed time to think. Her friends knew that.
She was grateful to them, for what they gave her in
their individual ways.

She missed Arturo. She missed him more than she
had known it was possible to miss another human
being. Even his silence was better than his absence.
Anything was better than his absence.

He was due to come home on Friday evening. The
seminar was finishing on Friday lunchtime. On
Thursday night, however, he phoned and told Carol
that he would be away an extra day. He said there was
someone he had to talk to, a man who lived in San
Francisco. It would be a long drive home. Arturo
would be back, he said, either Saturday night or Sunday
morning.

Carol hung up the phone, feeling sick. She smiled
brightly at Paul and explained that Arturo had business
to attend to. Maybe he had. And maybe Sonia Landis
was joining him for the weekend. She couldn't have
been there all week; she couldn't have stayed with him
in his hotel. Arturo wouldn't risk the gossip among his
contemporaries. But the weekend was a different matter
entirely, they could be staying together in a motel
somewhere, anywhere.

By Saturday night there was nothing left to do in the
house, it was completely in order. It was spotless. Carol
let her little brother stay up later than usual and
watched television with him, putting him to bed when

he fell asleep on her knee. Then she walked around the house like a lost soul, feeling no joy, no satisfaction as a result of all her efforts.

Arturo didn't come home. At a little after midnight she gave up and went to bed. It would be stupid to wait up half the night in the hope that he might come back. He had the perfect excuse for a weekend away with Sonia, hadn't he? She wondered, vaguely, what story Sonia would have given to her husband.

The irony was that she did not see Sonia Landis as a threat to her marriage. She herself was the threat. There was once a time when she would have been able to turn a blind eye to her doubts, or the reality, of what was going on. She had turned a blind eye to so much, mainly her husband's uncommunicativeness. But she hadn't loved Arturo then. At least, she hadn't realised it then. So everything had been that much easier to cope with.

Now, though, she felt drained. Her inner strength had gone. All she had now was a heart which ached with love, for love. A love that would never be given to her. How much longer could she carry on like this? How much more could she be expected to give—for Paul's sake?

For Paul's sake? Everything had started to boomerang as far as Paul was concerned. She had seen the boy return to his former self, being bright and chatty and happy. And now? Now he must be feeling as insecure as Carol was feeling.

Arturo came home just after lunchtime on Sunday. The extension to the garage had not been finished, and she watched from her bedroom window as he parked his car on the driveway. She smoothed down the skirt of her dress nervously and took a quick look in her mirror. She had put on a little make-up in an effort to look brighter because even she, now, couldn't deny that the strain was showing on her face.

Greeting her husband was like meeting a stranger. He, too, looked strained. Was it guilt? Did he have a conscience about the way he had spent his weekend? Or was it simply a result of the work he had been doing at the seminar?

'Hi.' She made herself smile as they came face to face, but even she heard the hollowness in her voice. 'You—didn't manage to get home last night after all.'

'I almost made it,' he muttered, following her into the living room. 'Had a blow-out on the freeway, and my spare tyre was flat. I had to stay the night in a motel just north of San Fernando. Where's Paul?'

'In his den.'

'I'll go and say hello.' He looked round the room, his expression telling her nothing. 'Then maybe you'd like to show me round?'

'Of course.' Like showing a guest round a hotel, she thought. What sort of atmosphere did this house have? How had it struck Arturo when he had walked through the front door?

The ground floor was open-plan, split-level. She called his name as he reached the stairs. 'Arturo——' He turned and she searched his face, not quite knowing what she was looking for. It was on the tip of her tongue to ask him whether he'd been with Sonia, but she found that she couldn't. The words stuck in her throat. What good would it do? If he had been with Sonia, his admission would only give Carol more pain. And if he hadn't, he would just be angry with her for suspecting him after he had told her the affair was finished.

'I was just wondering how your . . . your business in San Francisco went?'

'I won't have the answer to that for about a week.' With which he went upstairs and spent an hour with Paul.

He did not elaborate later, before they looked over the house, and Carol left the subject alone. It was an oddly-shaped house and Carol had liked that about it; they had both liked that. Arturo's study, which housed some of the furniture from the living room of the apartment, was on the first floor, next to Paul's bedroom, a guest room and one of the bathrooms. The main bedrooms and the other two bathrooms were on the top floor. Those, and a boxroom which was now full of empty cartons.

Arturo nodded as she showed him round, presumably in approval, but he made hardly any comments, much to her dismay. After dinner he went into his study and spent the rest of the evening there, ostensibly to sort out his papers. At midnight, when there was still no sign of him emerging, Carol went to bed without disturbing him.

She had by no means forgotten the advice Max had given her and she realised it was probably good advice since it was based on Max's knowledge of Arturo. But the more she thought about it, the more she was forced to admit that the idea of broaching the subject of Tessa frightened her, actually frightened her.

She had seen the pain in his eyes when he had mentioned her name. She had seen the anger when she had tried to make him talk about it. Still, she might have tried, tonight, to broach the subject—if he hadn't locked himself away in his study. It couldn't be more obvious that he had no wish to talk, about anything.

Really, Carol's thinking had got her nowhere. When she did manage to reach a conclusion, a decision about what she wanted to say to Arturo, one of two things happened: either she changed her mind because her courage deserted her or Arturo's attitude put her off. Tonight, his absence had made it impossible for her even to try.

Before getting undressed for bed, Carol took a long, hard look at herself in the mirror. How she had changed, in every conceivable way, from the person she had been six months ago! Where was the courage she once had in abundance? Where was that inner strength she could once rely on? Never had she been so pessimistic, so negative. Worry begets more worry, she had once reminded herself.

And so it had.

Four days later a letter for Arturo came from San Francisco. Before moving house, his mail had always been left at reception in Greenacres or sent to his offices in San Diego, depending on who was writing to him.

Carol put the envelope on the telephone table in the hall and looked at it without curiosity. She knew it concerned the visit Arturo had made to San Francisco after the seminar. So he had, after all, had a genuine reason for staying away from home. He hadn't been with Sonia Landis. That Carol could base all these conclusions merely on a postmark on an envelope was illogical, she knew. Yet she knew she was right.

It was Thursday. She was spending the morning at Greenacres and then she was going shopping. Arturo came into reception at lunchtime to take a look at the appointments book. Two patients had gone home that day and two new ones were due to arrive in the afternoon. Or rather, one new one and Sandy Goldman.

Sandy's road to recovery had been set back; she wasn't sick enough to be kept in a hospital of any kind and she wasn't well enough to go home. She had, however, allowed her mother to visit her after she had been in hospital a couple of days. Carol knew that that was a good sign.

'Well, there isn't a great deal for me to do this afternoon,' Arturo shrugged, addressing himself to Patti Morgan rather than to Carol.

'You're not complaining, Dr Kane?'

'No, Patti, indeed not.' He looked at Carol then. 'Maybe I'll collect Paul from school then take him out for a couple of hours, if that's okay with you?'

'Of course. I'm going shopping this afternoon. If—I can—I'll take my time about it now I know you're picking Paul up.' Dear Lord, what had she come to? She could hardly string a sentence together these days. She felt so nervous, so frightened. It was like living on top of a volcano and knowing it was going to erupt at any moment.

Arturo went into his office and Carol left just as Kay Sharpe arrived. Kay had been off duty for a couple of days and Carol hadn't spoken to her since the night of the emergency.

'Oh, Mrs Kane, how's everything at the new house?' Kay put down her small suitcase and straightened, looking self-confident and very attractive. She and Carol had almost established a rapport since Kay had stopped showing her resentment so much. She fancied Arturo like mad, Carol had known that all along, and no doubt the rest of the staff knew it, too. Only Arturo seemed oblivious to it. Whether he was or not was anyone's guess. One could never tell with Arturo.

'Fine, thanks. Everything's just fine,' How much longer, to how many more people, would she have to pay lip-service to those words, this pretence? 'Did you have a nice break, Kay? How was Palm Springs?'

'Relaxing, sunny. I feel better for the break. Well, if you'll excuse me, I'm back on duty in an hour.' She headed for the stairs as Carol turned to go, but not before Carol had noticed the curious look Kay had given her.

The boomerang, Carol thought as she drove away. It's happening in all directions. If things continued like this, the gossip Arturo had avoided by marrying the woman he was living with would start *because* he had married her. It was surely becoming obvious to everyone that the marriage had been a big mistake.

She drove into the heart of La Jolla and walked in and out of several shops and a supermarket in a total mental fog. She bought items in the supermarket which she knew she would never use, forgetting two essential things which necessitated her going back inside the place and having to queue all over again. She felt inordinately tired.

December was fast approaching and the shops were displaying Christmas gifts and goodies. It was raining.

There would be no snow at Christmas, it wasn't even cold here—although the Californians seemed to think so, from the way they were dressed.

On Herschel Avenue there was a rather smart coffee house Carol had been in many times with Nancy. She made a beeline for it and went straight into the ladies' room before ordering. . . . Only to find that her trials of the day were not yet over.

There were two other women in the ladies' room and one of them was Sonia Landis. Rightly or wrongly, Carol knew only a feeling of disgust as her eyes met with those of the other woman. It was probably wrong to feel like that since Sonia was no longer the 'other woman', but she couldn't help it. She looked away quickly and went into a cubicle.

Sonia Landis was waiting for her when she came out, however, and they were alone now. 'Mrs Kane——' Sonia's voice was tight with annoyance, her Southern drawl sounding clipped, almost foreign to Carol's ears.

Carol filled a basin with water. 'La Jolla isn't a big place,' she said crisply, unable to keep her tone neutral. 'It's feasible that we'll bump into one another from time to time. But I really don't think we have anything to say to each other.'

'I don't agree.' Sonia's blue eyes locked on to hers via the mirror over the wash-basin. Her irritation was very plain indeed. 'This is the second time you've looked at me as if I were the lowest thing on earth. I'd like to know why.'

Carol almost laughed at that. 'I'm in no mood for games, Mrs Landis.'

'I'm not playing games,' came the sharp reply. 'Look, when we met at the hairdresser's, it was—as you made certain—very obvious to me that you knew of my affair with Arturo. I can't imagine that he'd told you about me, described me, that isn't his style. But you'd worked it out somehow.' She paused, her tone softening slightly. 'I've never had an affair with your husband, Carol. Not with your *husband*. We were both free at the time—unattached and free to do as we wished.'

Unconsciously, Carol's eyes moved to Sonia's wedding ring.

'I'm a widow. My husband died two years ago—that's when I moved out here.'

'I—see. I'm sorry.'

'I wonder,' came the retort. 'I wonder what you're sorry about. You thought I had a husband, is that it?' She looked confused, but Carol didn't help her work things out. 'Even if I had a husband, I can't see you concerning yourself over my morality.'

There was a pause, and Sonia kept right on staring at Carol as she dried her hands. Carol had never been concerned about Sonia Landis' morality. She hadn't even been concerned about Arturo's . . . *morality*. There had been a period when, believing Sonia had a husband, Carol was glad the woman was not free. The knowledge had given her just a little bit of security.

Her total lack of security now, however, had nothing to do with Sonia Landis. She had worried herself sick over something which hadn't been happening. But that was nothing compared to her present worry. Any day now, Arturo would ask her to leave, she felt sure of it. Things just couldn't go on as they were.

'What did Art tell you about me, exactly?' Sonia demanded.

'Nothing,' Carol said wearily. 'Absolutely nothing.' She couldn't stand much more. Pretending was becoming impossible. 'That day you phoned, when Arturo came home late, I just put two and two together. I confronted Arturo with it and he said I needn't worry about it any longer.'

'Didn't he tell you he'd finished it between us?'

'He—implied it.'

'Is that all?' She laughed suddenly, humourlessly. 'I suppose that's typical of him.'

Carol found this familiarity with Arturo sickening, coming from her. She made no comment.

'If it's any consolation to you, you might be interested to know I'm working my notice at the hospital. Or has Art already told you that? I'm going home to Arkansas. So I won't even be seeing him in the course of duty for much longer.'

There was no nastiness in Sonia's voice, the tension had gone from it completely. 'When I learned Art had married, nobody could have been more surprised. He realised that when I talked to him, because he went on to explain about the boy, your brother, and that you'd married purely for his sake. Of course I knew damn well Art hadn't got married because he'd fallen madly in love! I know him very well, you'll appreciate that. After all, I'd been seeing him for almost a year. . . . Nevertheless, he finished with me when he married you.'

There was a touch of bitterness in the last few words. Enough to make Carol realise what this was all about. 'You're in love with him, aren't you, Sonia? That's why you're leaving California.'

Sonia's laugh was short. 'Wrong. I'm going home because I can't settle here. No, I'm not in love with your husband. I never was. It was just sex.' She said it bluntly, deliberately. 'We had a very private arrangement which suited us both.'

Then why the bitterness? Carol wondered. 'But before she had a chance to put the question, it was answered for her.

'I still want him, Carol. Is that honest enough for you? It's part of the reason I'm leaving. I see him two days a week and when I see him, I want him.'

Carol felt sick, but in the face of such bluntness she found she had no answer.

'Of course, you wouldn't know how that feels, would you? Being his wife.'

Fumbling for support, Carol leaned against the basin. Little did she know, this woman who was taking so much for granted. There was no way she would answer that one, even if she could find her voice.

But Sonia Landis hadn't finished yet. 'There are two sides to Arturo. Outside the sheets, he's the coldest man I've ever met.'

The contrast she was drawing did not go un-appreciated by Carol. She felt sick, emotionally battered beyond recovery. Sonia was talking in such a matter-of-fact manner, without any thought of Carol's feelings. She wanted to scream at the woman to shut up, but she couldn't utter a sound. She wanted to vomit.

'So he's all yours, Carol, and you're welcome.' Sonia shook her head as she moved towards the door. Then she paused, considering, just as someone else came into the room. 'If I'd loved him, I wouldn't have let him go without a fight. Married or not. But I don't see how one can love a man who has no emotions. So good luck to you in your marriage of convenience! I don't envy you having to live with him one little bit!'

Carol wouldn't have answered, even if someone else hadn't come into the room. She had no choice but to stay where she was for a few minutes, no choice but to withstand the curious look from the newcomer when she came over to wash her hands. Not until Sonia Landis was well clear of the place would Carol go back to her car. She moved over to a chair near the full-length mirror, her legs almost giving way beneath her.

At least she had kept her dignity in the face of Sonia's—bluntness. She had told her nothing. Oh, but Sonia was wrong, so wrong, in thinking she knew Arturo well. She didn't know him at all. She might have been seeing him for almost a year, but she had learned not the first thing about him, that was obvious.

That thought struck home. It was immediately followed by another: a man who has no emotions. What nonsense! Hadn't she, Carol, once made the mistake of thinking the same thing? But she had known for a long time that it wasn't true, even before Max had confirmed it. And what had she done about it? What had she done with her knowledge?

Nothing.

She stood up then, daring to think there might be

hope if she could just *talk* to Arturo. In the reflection of the mirror, she thought she looked pathetic. She was pathetic.

'If I'd loved him,' Sonia had said, 'I wouldn't have let him go without a fight.'

Carol stared at her reflection, summoning what little was left of her courage. Unwittingly, Sonia Landis had done her a favour. She had shaken her out of this apathy, this fog. Come hell or high water she would talk to Arturo tonight whether he wanted it or not. She had to. One way or another something would be settled. She was by no means optimistic about the outcome but something, *something* had to give.

'Good luck to you, too, Sonia Landis,' she muttered as she left the ladies' room.

CHAPTER ELEVEN

CAROL'S resolve did not desert her when she got home. She had just finished putting all her shopping away when Arturo came in with Paul, and still her courage didn't waver. He always looked so different when he was off duty. He had changed into a pair of denims and a black roll-neck sweater, but he was still formidable.

The conversation over dinner was as difficult as ever. Of course she could say nothing to her husband until Paul had been put to bed. From time to time she glanced at him, seeing the tension in his features. That face, how very, very dear to her it was. It was a face so full of character, the handsomeness unaffected by the lines which had deepened slightly. Not for the first time, she found herself plunged into the past, to a time when she had sat in her mother's back garden and analysed Arturo's face mentally, feature by feature. Really, she had started to get to know him then. Right then. So much had happened between them, so much time had elapsed, and yet . . . and yet she still knew so little about him. It didn't make much sense.

As soon as she had settled Paul for the night, Carol knocked on the door of Arturo's study. He had been in there while she was bathing Paul but he wasn't in there now. He was in the living room. She came down the open staircase with her heart in her mouth and it was only then that her courage wavered.

'I have to talk to you.'

Carol took the rest of the stairs slowly, shocked. The words had come from Arturo, not from her, and her heart skipped a beat. She was frightened. The room was dimly lit and she switched on a second lamp, as if the soft glow of its light would help her to feel warmer inside.

'Yes. I—yes?' She sat down in the settee, opposite the matching armchair which he seemed to favour.

'Carol, I've had a letter from that friend of a friend in 'Frisco. Or colleague of a colleague, rather.'

'I—saw a letter from San Francisco, yes.' She had no idea who had sent the letter, though.

'My offer has been accepted.' Arturo looked at her expectantly, his mouth set in an attitude she couldn't interpret for the moment.

'Arturo, I don't know what you're talking about. You told me over the phone that you were going to see someone in San Francisco, but you didn't tell me why.'

'I didn't?' He looked genuinely confused then. 'I— thought I . . . never mind.'

Carol's eyes closed briefly. His control was slipping. There was no mistaking that he was as uptight as she. It was stamped all over his face. He got up, too agitated to remain seated. 'At the seminar, I was told of someone who might be interested in joining me as a fourth partner in the practice. I called the guy and he invited me to his home to talk about it. He's newly qualified, newly married and he was very interested. I told him he could have the apartment at Greenacres. He wanted to talk it over with his wife, take a few days to think about it.'

'And now he's written and accepted your offer.' Carol wasn't sure where this was leading. 'Well, that's good news. It'll take some of the pressure off you.'

Arturo was standing with his back to her, his hands deep inside his trouser pockets. Suddenly he turned around. 'It means I'll be able to see more of Paul.'

'Yes.' Her voice was dull. Another partner could make quite a difference. Was he trying to tell her that he would be able to manage without her when he had more time? With an ordinary housekeeper, perhaps. . . .

In a voice which sounded strangely unlike him, he said, 'We made an arrangement, Carol, and you've stuck to it absolutely. You've been—admirable. This house—I like it very much. You've made it into . . .

what could be a very lovely home. But it isn't that, is
it?'

'No.'

'And Paul is being adversely affected by the strain
between us.'

'Yes.'

'And you—you're thinking of leaving.' It was
another statement, not a question.

Carol stared at him. Was everything, but everything,
going back to square one? Would he tell her next that
she couldn't have Paul? 'Is that what you want,
Arturo?'

He didn't answer. He turned away again. Carol felt
as though her heart were bleeding. The chips were
down. She had nothing to lose by telling the truth, by
telling him exactly how she felt. 'No, I'm not thinking
of leaving. If that's what you want, you'll have to ask
me to go. I love you, Arturo. I'll never leave you of my
own accord.'

He turned, slowly, and looked at her in disbelief.
'You—what?'

'I love you.' She said it almost brazenly, defiantly,
even as tears stung at the back of her eyes. But she did
not look away from him. 'And I'll never leave you of
my own accord.'

Silence reigned for what seemed like an eternity. He
couldn't seem to assimilate what she'd told him. 'But
you're unhappy!' he said at length. 'If you—why are
you so unhappy? Why are things so bad between us?
Why—how can you love a man like me?'

A cry escaped from her. A cry of protest, of
frustration. Did he not know his own worth? He had
always been oblivious to his attractiveness, but did he
not even know about his own worth?

Carol's heart was thumping wildly. Was this all he
had to say? He was *still* asking questions instead of
telling her how he felt. 'Do you know something,
Arturo? Since the time you once told me all the negative
aspects of love, I think this is the first time you've used

the word, in any context. I can't define my love for you.
I can't list the reasons. I just love you. But you are the
cause of my unhappiness. Why are you like this? *Why?*'

'Carol. . . .?'

She knew he was suffering. He knew very well what
she meant. She simply had to make him talk. Though she
wanted to go to him, to put her arms around him, she
didn't move. She was too afraid of driving him further
inside himself. 'Trust me,' she said instead. 'Please,
please trust me. Tell me about Tessa.'

He sat down, heavily, wearily, looking just as tired as
Carol was feeling. The ebony eyes searched her face
until, a moment later, he started talking. He finally
started talking and he kept on talking until Carol
reached a point when she thought he'd never stop. 'I
married Tessa when I was an intern at a big teaching
hospital in 'Frisco. In those days I had no interest, no
intention of going on to specialise in psychiatry. I was
going to practise general medicine and I couldn't wait
to get through with my internship and get started.

'She was very young—eighteen. Hell, we were both
young. I think we fell in love on sight. She was a
painter, or a would-be painter. I met her in the park
just across from the hospital. She was with a few other
artists, trying to sell her work.'

He smiled, and Carol closed her eyes against the sight
of it. Yes, he had loved Tessa very much.

'She was intelligent and very beautiful. She was also
moody, temperamental. At least, that's what I thought
it was. I hardly knew what the term manic-depressive
was in those days. I put her moods down to her artistic
temperament, to her frustration because she wasn't
making much progress in her work. Her work was very
important to her, I knew that from the start. She'd
come to California hoping to make her fortune. She
came from a poor family, a big family, in New York. She
wasn't strong physically, the climate here had also
been part of the lure.

'We married when I was still an intern. I was working

all the hours God sends, which is an intern's lot. Often I didn't get back to our apartment at night. She was alone so . . . too. . . .'

He stopped, and Carol had to look away from his eyes. Otherwise she couldn't have pressed him to continue. She was hurting for him, with him. 'Go on,' she said quietly.

'She . . . dear God, I didn't recognise what her moods meant. The times she was high, she. . . . And then when she . . . I came home one day and found her dead. She was five months pregnant.'

'I—Arturo——'

'It's all right,' he said quietly, calmly. 'It was a long time ago, Carol. Believe it or not, it doesn't hurt any more.'

She didn't believe it. But she understood. Oh, she understood so much more now he had told her all this. The glimpses she had had of the man behind the cool veneer, the pieces of the puzzle which had been Arturo Kane, all came together to make a whole. 'There is nothing,' Max had said, 'No human condition or emotion that he cannot understand and sympathise with. His feelings, his passions, run very deep.'

But Arturo had had insufficient technical knowledge in Tessa's day. He hadn't recognised her sickness, and he blamed himself for that. And what—how must it feel when a loved one takes their life? No wonder he didn't appreciate his worth; Tessa had deserted him in the most hurtful, irrevocable way. Just as his mother had hurt him by giving him away when he was a child. For what? Because she couldn't cope after her husband died? Because she had another man, perhaps? Someone who wasn't prepared to take on a child? It didn't really matter, except to acknowledge the effect it had had on Arturo.

Carol watched him as he poured out a couple of drinks. She felt proud, joyous because he had finally stripped himself of those barriers. It meant he trusted her. She could hope for nothing more than that. But it meant, at least, that he trusted her. It was something to cling to.

'Thank you.' She took the glass from him and he sat down beside her. 'You—became interested in psychiatry after—after this?'

'Yes. But I almost drank myself to death first. Max came to my rescue. He wasn't in California at the time. He was away, studying. He was two years ahead of me. He came back and found me—found a total wreck. Between him and Sam . . . well, they brought me back to normal eventually. After that,' he shrugged, 'I went from strength to strength. Max met Nancy shortly after he came back to California and—that's the whole story, I guess.'

'It's not the whole story,' Carol said quietly. She put down her glass and turned to face him squarely. 'If someone—a patient—came to you with a story like this. Oh, dear. . . .' She sighed, frustrated because she couldn't find the right words. 'Arturo, if you met a man who was only half alive emotionally, who never showed his feelings, who never volunteered what was going through his mind, and that man told you his story, this story, what conclusions would you reach?'

'The same conclusions you're reaching now.'

She looked at him worriedly. 'You mean, you can actually stand back and look at this? You're aware of the effect that Tessa and your mother had on you?'

'Of course I'm aware of it.' When he smiled, Carol thought it the saddest thing she had ever seen. 'They say that doctors are their own worst patients. That's one of the reasons they never treat themselves. It applies to psychiatrists, too. But Max has talked to me in the past. He's talked himself blue in the face. There's nothing I don't know about the theory, Carol. I am . . . was . . . half alive, as you say. I sealed up my emotions behind a very thick screen.'

'But knowing this hasn't helped you to. . . . You've still gone through all these years trying to avoid emotional enslavement. That's what you once called love. It's a phrase you've used more than once.'

'Have I?'

'Yes. You used it the night I—the night we made love.'

'When you virtually accused me of using me.'

'Yes, but . . . well, I've always regretted saying what I said.'

'But you meant it, Carol.'

'Yes.' She had regretted voicing her feelings, but she had meant what she had said. There was no point in lying to him. Not now. 'Arturo, I was in love with you even then. I wanted to thrash out at you for—what I thought you were doing to me.'

'So you had no idea how much I wanted you, how I felt about you?'

Carol's heart started hammering again, but still it was as a result of fear. What did he feel, exactly? Anything? Anything more than physical attraction?

When he moved away from her suddenly, her heart almost slowed to a stop. She began to feel faint. She had bared her soul, and now what? Did he think her a fool?

He was back in his armchair. At a safe distance. 'Carol,' he said quietly, so quietly she had to strain to hear him, 'I was emotionally involved with you long before I made love to you. But even if that hadn't been the case, I would have taken you to bed at the first opportunity. I make no apologies for finding you physically exciting. I wanted you. I wanted you from the first time I kissed you that time in San Francisco, even though at that particular moment sex was the last thing on my mind. When we married, I thought it would happen inevitably. But you were so cool, so——' he smiled at what he was about to say, 'so uninterested.'

She had to admire his honesty. She might have laughed because she had thought *him* uninterested. She might have laughed at the way she had avoided him, bristled when he had touched her. She might have laughed at the question he had asked her that day in the kitchen, when he had kissed her in earnest. But she couldn't laugh. All she could think of was him saying he was emotionally involved.

'Carol, I was devastated by what you said the night we made love. I was convinced you hated me for it. I felt as if I'd cheated you all along the line. I wasn't . . . able . . . to tell you how I felt about you. I didn't *want* to be emotionally involved.' He raked his fingers through the thick blackness of his hair, impatient with himself. 'But I am! God knows, I am! From the start I—somehow I knew it would happen . . . somewhere inside me, I knew. . . .'

She started to cry. She looked at him, listened to his struggle, and started to cry and to laugh at the same time. She crossed the room swiftly and he stood to take her in his arms. 'Don't do that. Don't cry—I can't stand it. Why are you crying?'

'Oh, my darling,' she blurted, 'it's because I'm happy. Don't you know anything?'

Arturo put a hand under her chin, the ebony eyes almost frantic as they looked into hers. 'I know I need you.' It was almost a whisper. 'Did you mean what you said, Carol? That you'll never leave me?'

For a moment she could only nod, but she struggled to find her voice, realising that he needed reassurance, as much as she could give. 'Yes, I meant it. I'll never leave you. Never!'

She watched his eyes, knowing that never again would they be able to keep secrets from her, seeing for herself how very deep his feelings went.

'I need you,' he said again. 'I need you so much.'

They clung together tightly and she rested her head against the broadness of his chest. He had almost managed to say it. Soon, she knew, he would be able to. Soon he would tell her in words that which his eyes had already told her.

For the moment she would be content in just knowing that he loved her.

SIX MAGNIFICENT SOLITAIRE DIAMOND RINGS FROM JAMES WALKER MUST BE WON **EACH WORTH £1,000** IN THE **MILLS & BOON**

Romantic Partners COMPETITION

Larger than actual size

Simply study the nine famous names from literary romances listed A to I below and match them (by placing letter in the appropriate box) to their respective partners. Then in not more than 12 words complete the tie breaker in an apt and original manner, fill in your name and address, together with the store where you purchased this book and send it to:

Mills & Boon Romantic Partners Competition 6 Sampson Street, London E1 9NA.

The six winners will each receive a magnificent solitaire diamond ring, worth* £1,000 (retail value) specially selected from the wide range available at James Walker the jewellers.

*Correct at time of going to print as valued by James Walker, Jewellers.

RULES

WORTH £1,000 (retail value)

ENTRY FORM:—

1. Dr Zhivago &
2. Maria &
3. Rochester &
4. Heathcliff &
5. Antony &
6. Nelson &

A. Juliet
B. Lara
C. Josephine
D. Rhett Butler
E. Emma Hamilton
F. Baron Von Trapp
G. Cleopatra
H. Cathy
I. Jane Eyre

Tie Breaker:— Mills & Boon is the very best in romantic fiction because (complete this sentence in not more than 12 words):

....

....

NAME (BLOCK CAPITALS PLEASE) ....

ADDRESS ....

BOOK PURCHASED AT ....